Praise for *The Beloved Daughter* by Alana Terry

Grace Awards, First Place

IndieFab Finalist, Religious Fiction

Women of Faith Writing Contest, Second Place

Book Club Network Book of the Month, First Place

Reader's Favorite Gold Medal, Christian Fiction

"...an engaging plot that reads like a story out of today's headlines..." ~ Women of Faith Writing Contest

"In this meticulously researched novel, Terry gives readers everything a good novel should have — a gripping story, an uplifting theme, encouragement in their own faith, and exquisite writing." ~ Grace Awards Judges' Panel

"The Beloved Daughter is a beautifully written story." ~ Sarah Palmer, Liberty in North Korea

There was silence for such a long time Kennedy wondered if there was a problem with Carl's antique cell phone. Finally, Rose asked, "And so what happens if you get pregnant, and you're too young to actually have a baby?"

Defying all laws of inertia, the acceleration of Kennedy's heart rate crashed to a halt like a car plowing into a brick wall. "What do you mean?"

"Like, what if you're too young but you still get pregnant?"

"How young?" Kennedy spoke both words clearly and slowly, as if rushing might drive the timid voice away for good.

"Like thirteen."

Praise for *Unplanned*
by Alana Terry

"Deals with **one of the most difficult situations a pregnancy center could ever face**. The message is **powerful** and the story-telling **compelling**." ~ William Donovan, *Executive Director Anchorage Community Pregnancy Center*

"Alana Terry does an amazing job tackling a very **sensitive subject from the mother's perspective**." ~ Pamela McDonald, *Director Okanogan CareNet Pregnancy Center*

"**Thought-provoking** and intense ... Shows **different sides of the abortion argument**." ~ Sharee Stover, *Wordy Nerdy*

"Alana has a way of sharing the gospel **without being preachy**." ~ Phyllis Sather, *Purposeful Planning*

How can you fall in love with someone you've never met?

Susannah's convinced that God has called her to the mission field. That's why she's serving him with single-minded focus in Orchard Grove, waiting for the day when she can leave her small town to take the gospel to the nations. Is falling in love with her missionary recruiter part of God's plan for her life or a distraction from the real goal?

Scott loves his life. Traveling the globe, offering spiritual support to missionaries around the world offers enough excitement that the loneliness hardly ever gets to him ... Until he receives an application from a young girl with a heart for the mission field as large as his own, a young girl he finds himself falling for even before they get the chance to meet face-to-face.

Unfortunately, a promise Susannah made to her family may tear her and Scott even farther apart than the miles that separate them.

Praise for *What Dreams May Come* by Alana Terry

*"God loves us, has our best in mind, and has **VERY good plans for us**. What dreams God has in store for you my friend....read this precious story, and dare to dream!" Barbara Carter*

*"It's **so refreshing** to read a love-filled Christian romance that shows God's hand in our lives!" Jan Carney*

*"This story is **beautifully written**." Darlene Napier Richter, Book Reviewer*

Simon exhaled as he stretched his arms. "I wish we didn't have to say good-bye." His voice was distant.

Hannah stared at the moon. She would never sit here beside him again in this garden. "There are no good-byes in the kingdom of heaven," she whispered, hoping her words carried the conviction her soul lacked.

Praise for *Torn Asunder*
by Alana Terry

"Filled with suffering, yet ultimately has a **resounding message of hope**." ~ Sarah Palmer, Liberty in North Korea

"Alana has a **great heart for the persecuted church** that comes out in her writing." ~ Jeff King, President of International Christian Concern

"Faith and love are tested beyond comprehension in this **beautifully written Christian novel**." ~ Kathryn Chastain Treat, Allergic to Life: My Battle for Survival, Courage, and Hope

"**Not your average love story** - wrapped in suspense, this story of faith will stop your heart as you hope and weep right along with the characters." ~ Nat Davis, Our Faith Renewed

"Torn Asunder is an **enthralling, heart-aching novel** that calls your heart to action." ~ Katie Edgar, KTs Life of Books

She shook her head. *"I don't know. I can't say. I just know that something is wrong here. It's not safe."* She clenched his arm with white knuckles. *"Please, I can't ... We have to ..."* She bit her lip.

He frowned and let out a heavy sigh. "You're absolutely certain?"

She nodded faintly. "I think so."

"It's probably just nerves. It's been a hard week for all of us." There was a hopefulness in his voice but resignation in his eyes.

She sucked in her breath. "This is different. Please." She drew her son closer to her and lowered her voice. *"For the children."*

"All right." He unbuckled his seatbelt and signaled one of the flight attendants. *"I'm so sorry to cause a problem,"* he told her when she arrived in the aisle, *"but you need to get my family off this plane. Immediately."*

Praise for *Turbulence*
by Alana Terry

"This book is **hard to put down** and is a **suspenseful roller coaster of twists and turns**." ~ Karen Brooks, *The Book Club Network*

"I've enjoyed all of the Kennedy Stern novels so far, but **this one got to me in a more personal way** than the others have." ~ *Fiction Aficionado*

"I love that the author is **not afraid to deal with tough issues all believers deal with**." ~ Kit Hackett, *YWAM Missionary*

Note: The views of the characters in this novel do not necessarily reflect the views of the author, nor is their behavior necessarily condoned.

Breath of Heaven
Copyright © 2017 Alana Terry
ISBN 978-1-941735-48-0
December, 2017

Cover design by Victoria Cooper.

www.alanaterry.com

Breath of Heaven

a novel by Alana Terry

CHAPTER 1

I'll wait a little longer. Then I'll tell him.

Katrina tucked a stray strand of hair behind her ear and listened at the door of her husband's study.

"Absolutely. It'll be done before church tomorrow."

Who was he on the phone with now? And was this one of those calls that would age him another five years?

"Yeah, it was just that we ran out of salt the night before, and I forgot to get some from the store … You're right. It was slippery. I'm just glad no one was hurt."

Katrina bit the corner of her lip, trying to guess who would have called to complain. Unfortunately, the suspect list was at least a dozen names long.

"I'm very sorry about that," Greg was saying. Funny how he had apologized to every single member of the congregation in the past six months, but never to her.

Not even once.

"I've already asked Katrina to add it to the shopping list … Yeah, I'll tell her to get two. That's a good idea."

The parsonage was so cold Katrina was surprised she couldn't see her own breath. Greg insisted on keeping the thermostat set at sixty to save the church any extra expense. One less thing for him to apologize over at those monthly business meetings while the treasurer read over the line items of the budget.

The door opened. "What're you doing here, Mouse?"

Since she first met him as a teen in his youth group, Greg had been making her heart leap. She fidgeted with the small gold band of her wedding ring. "I was just … I was on my way to …"

Greg's study sat at the end of an otherwise unused hall. Katrina threw her glance toward the pantry on the opposite side. "I was looking to see if we had any cans of cream of mushroom left."

Greg frowned. The expression fell so naturally on his face.

Katrina bit her lip. "How's everything going?" She wondered what it would be like to for once feel at home in her own house. Orchard Grove Bible Church's house, actually. Certain members of the congregation liked to point out at every single business meeting how generous the church was to let the young pastor and his bride live there rent free. So why, they asked, was it so hard for the newlyweds to keep the walkways shoveled now that the snow was falling?

Greg stared past her shoulder. "Fine."

"Who was on the phone?" She regretted asking the question as soon as the words left her mouth.

His jaw tightened. "Oh, it was nothing."

She'd learned enough over the past six months that she didn't ask for more information. They had moved to Orchard Grove right after their wedding, hopped in the car once the ceremony ended and honeymooned on the road from southern California to apple country, Washington. Not that Orchard Grove wasn't pretty. It had a certain desert-like appeal, if you liked dry landscapes with plenty of rocks. The orchards were out of town, which would make for some nice Saturday drives if Greg actually got the weekends off.

Orchard Grove was colder than anything she had experienced in Long Beach, but she and Greg were trying valiantly to master shoveling snow, salting sidewalks, and driving on sheets of solid ice like everyone else. She tightened her sweater around her and let her eyes linger for a second or two on the thermostat dial. A quick turn, two or three degrees at most. But by the time Greg finished lecturing her about stewardship and a pastor's obligations for fiscal responsibility, the extra heat wouldn't warm her anyway.

"Are you ready for the decorating party?" Greg asked. It was strange how much mumbling he did at home, but as soon as someone called on the phone or he went to preach from the pulpit, his diction was clear as a newscaster's.

Katrina pictured herself as she had rehearsed, spine erect, eyes focused, her entire being exuding confidence as she explained why she had chosen to stay home instead of helping the Women's Missionary League hang lights and various greeneries around the sanctuary and foyer of Orchard Grove Bible Church.

"Well?" Greg leaned forward slightly, holding his hand to the doorframe as if his study were a vacuum ready to suck him back in at a moment's notice. "You did remember that's today, didn't you?"

Katrina straightened her back. She mentally listed all the logical reasons that would excuse her from an afternoon with the ladies of Orchard Grove, the hordes of bustling, gossiping, back-biting biddies that seemed to make up the bulk of the Missionary League. She sucked in her breath. "I'm just running a little late. I'll be ready as soon as I change my clothes."

Greg was halfway back in his study before muttering, "You should probably wear your skirt or a dress or something. Don't forget what happened last time."

As if Katrina ever could.

"Yeah, I'll see you this afternoon. I was thinking of using up the leftover chicken for dinner tonight."

Greg didn't respond. Katrina dragged her bare feet down the hall as her husband's cell called him away. The sound of his ringtone laughed at her from behind his closed door.

CHAPTER 2

"Katrina, dear, that color goes absolutely stunning with your complexion," exclaimed one of the women at the church. Several other ladies from the Missionary League voiced their agreement.

"You're such a tiny little thing." Rotund Mrs. Porter pouted and reached out a finger to stroke Katrina's jawline. "And Pastor Greg, he must be a foot taller than you!"

Katrina forced a smile.

"You really should have saved that blouse for the Christmas Eve service." Mrs. Porter rubbed the fabric of Katrina's collar. "You'd look perfectly exquisite standing there with your violin in front of the tree." She turned to the other women for confirmation. "Wouldn't she look exquisite?"

Murmurs of agreement assaulted Katrina's ears. She fidgeted with her wedding ring, twisting the plain band around her finger, wondering how to divert attention away from her size, her blouse, her music.

"We've been so excited to hear you play again." Mrs. Porter gave her shoulder an uninvited rub. "It's not right for you to make us wait so long. You haven't forgotten anything, have you?" Her smile sent a cold shudder racing up Katrina's spine.

Another woman wrapped her arm around Katrina's waist. "How could she forget? Playing a violin is just like riding a bike, isn't it, dear?"

Katrina stared longingly at the boxes of Christmas decorations stacked in neat rows in the foyer. She pictured herself walking up to the closest one, tearing off the tape, and emptying its contents but instead held perfectly still, as immobile as the gaudy Christmas tree in the sanctuary.

"What are you going to play for us Christmas Eve?" Mrs. Porter asked, and several women broadcasted their suggestions.

Nancy Higgins, the church treasurer, offered a soft smile. "A girl has the right to keep a secret or two around here, hasn't she?"

If Katrina hadn't been so keenly aware of the League women staring at her, she might have rolled her eyes. Secrets. At a place like Orchard Grove Bible Church? The thought was too absurd to be funny. Two months before the wedding, she and Greg flew from Long Beach to

Washington to show the members of Orchard Grove Bible why he was the best pastoral candidate for their church. She had no idea the congregation would scrutinize her just as thoroughly. They seated Katrina and Greg in front of the sanctuary and barraged them with questions. When were they saved? Did either of them struggle with lust? Had they kept themselves pure during their entire engagement?

The fact that Katrina played violin with the Long Beach Symphony Orchestra caused a bigger stir than she would have expected if Greg confessed to being a drug addict. *Of course you'll lead worship*, everyone assumed, even though both she and Greg explained more than once that she didn't sing. And the questions. *With music being such a big part of your life, could you adjust to our little rural town? Do you plan to teach lessons? You do realize there's no orchestra here, don't you? Won't you die of boredom?* It had been Nancy Higgins who asked that, and now looking back, Katrina wondered if the woman had been giving her a warning.

The first Sunday of Greg's new job, Mrs. Porter had stared at Katrina while she walked the entire fifty feet from the front door of the parsonage to the church entrance. "And where is your violin?" she demanded. Katrina had no idea the congregation expected her to play her very first Sunday, but Mrs. Porter and a vocal number of others insisted until Greg asked her to run home and grab her case.

Now, with Mrs. Porter's arm tucked stalwartly around her waist, Katrina couldn't even remember what song she had performed that day. It had felt so forced. So crude. A violation was how she explained it to Greg when they were safe at home after the service. He'd stared at her incredulously for a full ten seconds before asking if she was overreacting.

Now Katrina managed to slip her way out of Mrs. Porter's grasp so the old woman wouldn't feel her whole body tremble. Secrets. Well, there was one she still held. Last fall, Katrina had begged her husband to explain to the church that she needed a break from playing her violin. She feigned weakness in her wrists, not an outright lie. Even so, Greg had only managed to appease the disappointed masses with the promise that Katrina would play again at the Christmas Eve service.

What had he been thinking? It was too soon. She couldn't pick up her violin. Not after what happened.

Secrets.

Katrina tucked her hair behind her ears.

"Well now." Mrs. Porter clapped her hands, and the women of the Missionary League followed her like a flock of geese as they swarmed around the Christmas boxes. "We have a church to decorate."

CHAPTER 3

"What're you doing, Mouse?"

Katrina jerked her head up and shoved the photograph back into her diary. "Nothing." Her face burned hot. She fidgeted with her wedding band and glanced at the journal in her lap.

Greg unbuttoned the top few buttons of his shirt. Worry creases replaced the laugh lines that had first made her heart flutter when she was a student in his youth group so many years ago. She bit her lip. What had happened?

"How'd decorating go?" He dropped his shirt on the floor and changed into a faded Lakers jersey. "I didn't even hear you come home."

Her fingers thumped against her journal, burning hot with guilt. "It was fine. Everything looks really nice."

He sat on the edge of the bed and untied his shoes. This dressing down ritual each evening reminded her of Mr. Rogers, and she loved its peaceful monotony.

Greg stretched his arms above his head. He had lost most

of his tan with the move but not his athletic physique. Katrina sat an arm's length away from those strong, familiar shoulders. She could just reach out ...

"Oh, did I already ask you to pick up another bag of ice melt from the store?"

She searched his voice for signs of worry or strain, but he sounded surprisingly relaxed.

"I can do that."

She held her breath as he leaned toward her, felt her face flush. His kiss was short, a peck if you could even call it that, but the softness of his lips on hers whispered hints of promise. She placed her hand on his chest, ready if he decided to give her another kiss, a real one this time.

"That's a pretty shirt." He fingered the soft nylon. "Have I seen you wear it before?"

"Probably." She swept a strand of hair behind her ear, remembering the night years ago she had stayed late after the youth group Christmas party to help clean up. It was the first time she and Greg had ever been alone together. The first time she noticed his eyes held the same hopefulness, the same awkward embarrassment, the same frustrations that had stolen away any hope she had at a happy senior year of high school. It could never work. It wouldn't be right. Yet still she had worn the new blouse her mom picked out for her and stayed late to clean up, wondering if he'd notice her, hoping he'd realize she was a young woman and not another silly teenager.

Greg laced his fingers behind his head and stretched himself out on the bed. Katrina curled up beside him automatically. Waiting. Just like she had so many Christmases ago. So uncertain. Greg was staring at her. They had only been married for six months, but she knew that expression. Hope swelled up in the pit of her gut, clashing with fear. The two emotions warred against each other, churning her stomach.

"I love you, Mouse." Greg stroked her cheek.

She bit her lip and didn't trust her voice.

He locked into her stare. "You're so beautiful."

She shut her eyes. Tasted his sweet, soft lips. Let out her breath and sighed into him.

His legs intertwined with hers. "You're the best thing that's ever happened to me." His kisses caressed her chin, her neck, her shoulder.

A tinny refrain grated her ears. He reached for his cell phone, glanced at the screen, and set it back on the end table. "They can wait."

She relaxed in his arms. More like melted, really, as the phone protested with one more annoying whine and then fell silent.

CHAPTER 4

The chicken was burned, but neither of them mentioned it. She sat across from him at their small folding table, and every once in a while his bemused smile sent a flush spreading across her entire face.

"What?" she finally asked, almost choking on a bite of rice.

"I love you so much."

She couldn't raise her eyes to his.

"I still don't know how I ended up with a woman like you."

She stuffed a forkful of veggie casserole into her mouth.

Greg stretched his legs out beneath the table. "I can't believe things worked out like they did. You should have seen the pastor's face when I told him I was falling for one of the girls from my youth group." He chuckled.

Katrina took a sip of milk.

He reached out and grasped her hand, twisting the simple band on her ring finger. "And now you're all mine."

She smiled behind her napkin.

"It's gonna be our first real Christmas together, Mouse. You haven't even told me what to get you."

He had been pestering her for gift ideas for a month or more, and she still didn't know how to answer. "I'll need a new journal soon."

He chuckled. "Another? How many do you go through in a year?"

She tried to match his smile, but her stomach flipped itself into a series of pretzel knots. A growing, gnawing emptiness with no hope for reprieve.

He was rubbing her hand. Smiling at her. The worry lines were gone. The phone hadn't rung in over an hour. Christmas was less than a month away, their first Christmas together as husband and wife. It could be so perfect ...

He took a bite of chicken. Did he realize how dry it was? "If you need more gift ideas, I was thinking maybe Monday before the business meeting we could ..." A tinny, muffled ring. Color drained from his face. His eyes widened, and he thrust his hand into his pocket. "Shoot."

Katrina wondered how many of his congregants would be appalled to hear their pastor make such an innocuous exclamation.

He jumped up from the table. "I left my phone in the bedroom, Mouse. I'm sorry. I'll be right back."

Katrina took another bite of casserole.

Greg was apologizing into his cell when he returned. "I understand completely. I'm terribly sorry ... No, I just left my phone in the other room, that's all."

Katrina paused with her cup of milk in her hand.

"I'll be sure to let her know. Yes ... Yes, I understand the financial situation completely. I'm sure it was an innocent mistake. Of course she wouldn't have ... Ok. Well, you too. All right. Good night."

That familiar heaviness, the weary expression clouded Greg's face. "That was Mrs. Porter."

Katrina replayed Greg's side of the conversation in her mind, paying careful attention to his tone.

"I guess one of the ladies left the lights on downstairs this afternoon. She and her husband were driving past the church and saw it on."

"Why didn't they stop and turn it off?" Katrina mumbled into her napkin.

Greg didn't seem to hear. "Would you mind taking care of that after dinner?"

Katrina stared at the blackened chicken on her plate. "Fine." She hadn't meant to sound so terse.

Greg held up his hand. "Hey, if it's a big deal, I'll go do it right now."

"No." She reached out. "It's not a problem. I'll take care of it as soon as I clear the table."

Greg shrugged her hand off his shoulder. "Never mind. I'll handle it myself." He grunted as he stepped into his snow boots. "Sheesh, it's just a simple light. It's nothing to get so worked up about."

Just a simple light. Katrina wished more people at Orchard Grove Bible Church realized that as her husband clunked outside in his boots, slamming the door shut behind him.

CHAPTER 5

"Hey, Mouse, you feeling ok?"

Katrina shielded her eyes from the bedroom light. "What?" Her voice was groggy. She cleared her throat.

"I asked if you're feeling ok. I've never seen you sleep in so late."

She turned toward the clock but didn't want to uncover her eyes. "What time is it?"

"Five to nine."

She groaned. She had always been slow to wake up, which was even more annoying now that she was married. Half the time she couldn't remember if she and Greg had gone to bed angry at each other or not. What was their most recent blowup? There had to be something, right?

Oh, yeah. Those stupid church lights.

Greg was frowning. "You sick?" He swept some hair out of her face, and she forced herself to smile.

"I'm all right. Just tired." She made a show of sitting, but her lower abdomen tightened up as soon as she moved.

17

Great.

"Is something wrong?" he asked again.

She didn't mention the cramps. She didn't need him rolling his eyes at her *women problems,* and she certainly didn't want him going through the day thinking she was making excuses to get out of her responsibilities. Why did these things always have to happen on Sundays?

"I'll be out in a few minutes." She flashed her biggest smile to compensate for her discomfort and imagined how blissful it would feel to be the kind of woman who could sleep in on a Sunday for as long as she wanted. No pews to straighten up. No sanctuary to vacuum. No nursery workers to call …

Uh-oh.

"By the way, did you find another volunteer to go downstairs this week?" Greg asked.

She squeezed her eyes shut. She could handle this. In first grade, she had practiced her new violin so hard her fingers bled, but she hadn't stopped. She had kept playing, all the way through elementary school, junior high, and high school. All the way through two semesters of community college where she made enough money playing with the Long Beach Symphony Orchestra and teaching private lessons that she could have rented a small apartment of her own if her mom hadn't forbidden it. She had endured hours of rehearsals under ruthless conductors as arrogant as they were incompetent. She had fingered and bowed her way through orchestral politics and left the Long Beach Symphony without a single enemy to her name.

She had been so excited at the thought of leaving California. No more traffic jams. No more senseless violence. No more family drama. Moving to Orchard Grove with Greg had sounded like such an adventure, the first time she dared to embark on her own without her mom's disapproving stare following her everywhere she went. *Apple country.* That's how Greg had described the area, but now all she could see from the parsonage was the church, some worn-down apartments, and a dried-up riverbed.

Some view.

She hadn't expected to miss the orchestra so much. Sure, there was a kind of comradery that you could never replicate outside the rehearsal room or performance hall. Friends two or three times her age who nevertheless considered her an equal. Most of them had never met Greg, so she didn't have to worry about people referring to her as *the pastor's wife.* She was Kat, the second violinist. Stand partners with Stan, the Vietnam vet. She didn't remember when they started calling her Kat. She never invited them to, it just happened. *Kat.* Not Mouse or Katrina or *the pastor's wife.*

Kat.

Everyone called her that. Even Lyn — the forty-year-old conductor whose athletic body had attracted more young women to the symphony than any previous Long Beach maestro. *Kat, be careful. You're rushing the fourth movement. Kat, you're swaying so widely during the* adagio *section poor Stan has to dodge your bow.*

"You didn't forget, did you?"

Katrina stared at her husband dumbly.

"The nursery," he prompted. "Did you find a substitute?"

Her cheeks burned hot. "No." She was stammering as badly as a first-year violin student learning to play *spiccato.* "No, I mean, I didn't forget, but I figured I could go down there this time. It's almost my week anyway."

Another frown. "You know it's important for me to have you upstairs. For the church to see us together."

"Yeah, I know. I'll try to trade with somebody next time. That way I won't miss more than one this month."

"You could call Mrs. Porter. She doesn't seem to mind jumping in last minute."

Mrs. Porter didn't seem to mind jumping into anything at any time as long as it meant she got to boss people around or earned some recognition out of it when all was said and done. But Katrina kept the blasphemous thought to herself.

"I don't want to bother her. She's probably in the middle of getting ready for church."

Greg leaned into the doorframe. "What, you want me to call and ask?"

"No." Katrina rolled her eyes, but thankfully her husband didn't notice.

"You know, it would have been nice if you'd taken care of this last week when it first came up."

"I already said I'd do nursery today."

He turned his back to her. "Now I've got to call Mrs. Porter, and I'll have to listen to her complain about those stupid lights you left on downstairs ..."

Katrina had mentally gone over the Women's Missionary League decorating party a dozen times last night and knew with certainty that Mrs. Porter was the last woman to come upstairs after the boxes were put in storage, but she couldn't say that. Greg would just think she was being petty, and nobody else would care except for Mrs. Porter herself, who of course would deny it. For all the trouble that single light caused, Katrina would have preferred having the church treasurer dock seventy-five cents off Greg's next paycheck to cover the extra expense.

If it would even amount to that much.

CHAPTER 6

She wouldn't go to church today. It was as simple as that. She hadn't missed a Sunday yet, not even after everything that happened last fall. She had wanted to stay home then, but Greg talked her into going. Reminded her that church was like a family that you could turn to when you were hurting. Except nobody there knew about her pain. Even Greg forgot after those first few days.

She was still in bed, even though it was past the time she usually headed over. Greg was gone, spreading salt over the icy walkways and doing whatever else he did to get ready for the service. She would explain it to him when he came back, tell him about her cramps. Anything that hinted at *lady problems* sent her husband racing to the next county to avoid talking about uncomfortable issues. He might be disappointed about her missing church, and there was still the issue of nobody to work in the nursery, but it wouldn't be the first time a volunteer failed to show up without notice.

She deserved a break, didn't she? Just one week without

checking over her shoulder to make sure the nursery volunteer remembered to go downstairs after the singing. One week without Mrs. Porter reminding her of all the things that she had forgotten. Katrina's to-do list multiplied over Thanksgiving and was now five times its usual size and would stay that way until New Year's.

Her midsection seized up, firing pain through her hips and lower back. Thankfully she was just uncomfortable. No flashbacks, at least not yet. Even so, it would probably only be a matter of time.

She heard Greg's footsteps down the hall and rehearsed her excuse. He'd be disappointed, then he'd get over it. Sundays were stressful for him, that was all. It wouldn't be personal. He'd forget about it by next week.

The door crashed open and Greg plowed into the bedroom. "Where have you been?"

She sat up as quickly as she could, dismissing her plans to skip church as childish and lazy. Agony grabbed her entire torso and refused to release her.

Greg's scowl melted off his face. "Mouse, what's wrong? Are you sick?"

The next wave of cramps was strong enough to erase the sound of his voice until all she heard was the horrific beeping of the machine they had hooked her up to in the hospital to check her vitals last fall. She shut her eyes. Nurses. How many of them? Two? Three? Arguing about how much pain medication they were supposed to give. She was lying there bleeding out, and the only thing anyone cared about was whether the doctor had said five cc's or ten.

"Mouse, do you need to go to the hospital?"

He was holding her hand. Greg. Her Greg. The one she had agonized over so many restless nights. The one she had filled three whole journals writing about during her senior year of high school. Praying. Apologizing to God, ashamed of her emotions. Begging the Lord to take away her feelings. Reminding herself it was a stupid, ridiculous, unrequited crush.

Until she saw his eyes the night of the Christmas party. And now those same soft eyes were watching over her with a mixture of fear and pain. "Mouse, tell me what's wrong."

She blinked back tears. She had work to do. Of all the women in Orchard Grove who still menstruated, she wouldn't be the one to let a few cramps paralyze her for the day. She had duties at church. She was the nursery coordinator, and there was nobody else to watch those kids so their parents could worship properly. She was the pastor's wife. Her place was by Greg's side, greeting congregants, supporting her husband, praying for him from her seat in the front of the sanctuary.

"I'm ok."

He helped her out of bed. His touch was so strong. Protective. She wanted to hug him. Let him swallow her up in his arms. Lean her head against his chest and stay there all day, listening to his heartbeat. She thought about the night they chaperoned prom for the small Christian school in Long Beach. She was almost twenty years old, but it was the first school dance she'd ever attended. Even so, her mom probably wouldn't have let her go if she'd realized Greg would be there. If she realized what would happen that night. There were so many things her mom hated about Katrina. The way she couldn't hold a tune when she sang. The way she swayed too much when she played her violin. The way she fell in love with a penniless youth pastor.

He kissed the top of her head. "Cramps?"

She nodded.

"They bad?"

Another nod.

"Do you want to stay in bed?"

He was so good to her. She knew how tense he got before church service, but even now he was thinking about her well-being. She reached out for the black dress hanging in the back of their closet. "I'll be ok."

"You sure?"

Why couldn't things always be like this? Why couldn't he always be so compassionate? So caring? During their entire courtship and engagement, he had acted like a prince. Sending her sweet emails throughout the day. Buying her little trinkets whenever he was out just because he was thinking about her. Cooking dinner on the weekends, just the two of them. They'd stay up late playing board games or reading Narnia books to each other.

God, what happened?

She got herself dressed, and he didn't leave her side. He rubbed the small of her back where the pain radiated the most. She didn't deserve his love. Didn't deserve any of this.

"Do you want some Tylenol?"

She pulled on her nylons. "Yes, please."

"Anything for my Mouse."

He kissed her cheek and let his lips linger close to her mouth. She thought again of that night chaperoning the prom, how they had stayed late to take down decorations until they were the only two people left. She had seen that same hopefulness in his eyes that night too. That same hunger. Except this time, she wasn't a teenager in his youth group. This time, they were two adults, free to make their own decisions.

Free to fall in love.

She watched him leave as she slipped on her black heels. She hadn't realized it at first, but she was dressed in perfect concert attire. All black. No collars to get in the way of her chin rest. No ostentatious jewelry to distract the audience from her music. She wondered what her friends would be playing at the holiday pops concert. This would be the first Christmas she could remember without going, either as an audience member or part of the orchestra. Who sat in her seat now? Was it someone who got promoted up to her stand or a rookie? Could they turn the pages fast enough to satisfy Stan's grumpy demands?

Greg came back a few minutes later with two pills and a mug of Ovaltine. "Here you go."

He rubbed the back of her neck while she swallowed the Tylenol. The hot chocolate slipped down her throat and sent waves of heat rippling out from her stomach. "Thanks."

He bent down and kissed her forehead. "Any time. You sure you feel up for church today?"

She twisted her wedding band and glanced at her fingernails. How long had it been since she caressed the strings of her violin? "Yeah."

"I'll ask Mrs. Porter to take over nursery so you can just rest during the service."

"That's ok. I'll be all right." At least the rocking chair downstairs was more comfortable than the pews.

Another kiss. A lingering one. "I love you, Mouse."

"I love you too."

He wrapped his arm around her, and they walked together to the entryway where he draped her coat over her shoulders.

Katrina swallowed down the painful lump in her throat.

God, what happened?

CHAPTER 7

"Oh, there's someone here. I was worried."

Joy Holmes, one of the church's only young mothers, propped the nursery door open with her foot. She held her one-year-old baby, who was laughing at her own spit bubbles, in one arm and dragged her three-year-old inside while she tugged against her mom's firm grasp.

"Come on, Zoe. Let's go in and play." Her voice was breathy, as if she were winded from walking down the stairs. Or maybe she was trying to keep from losing her temper in front of the pastor's wife.

Zoe shook her head and let her legs fall beneath her.

"Do you want a timeout?" Joy demanded and shot an unconvincing smile at Katrina. "I'm sorry. She's in a mood today. Her father gave her and her brother too much pie at Thanksgiving, and I swear they're both still on a sugar high. She'll probably whine for a few minutes after I leave, but then …"

Joy set her baby down on the carpet. "Here you go,

Brielle. At least you know how to play quietly." Two seconds later Brielle had dumped out an entire bin full of cardboard bricks.

"Oh, these kids," Joy muttered.

"Must keep you busy." Katrina forced herself to smile as Brielle banged two bricks against the empty box. Katrina would love the chance to get to know Joy better, but she was so busy with her three children and had another on the way and always seemed to have a flustered, I'm-too-busy-to-be-bothered kind of air. She straightened up, and Katrina could see the swell of her pregnant belly.

"You don't know the half of it," Joy exclaimed with another long sigh. "I'm just thrilled we're not having twins. Ok, I'm taking off. I've got to get upstairs or I swear DJ's going to drive his father insane. That boy has way too much energy. Don't mind Zoe if she screams for a minute or two. She'll calm down after that and be fine."

Joy rested her hand on her abdomen, leaned over to give her daughters a hug, and waddled out the door. As soon as it shut, Zoe ran to it with a screech that would rival the sound of a first-time violin student.

What am I doing here? Katrina asked herself, eying the box of cheap, mismatched toys. Wasn't there something in there she could find to distract a three-year-old? The only problem was she ached so much she didn't want to get out of the rocking chair. She should be in bed. Not stuck here in this nursery. Another screech. She just needed the noise to stop.

"Come on, Zoe," she whispered, certain the child couldn't hear. "Want to go get a book? I'll read it to you in the rocker."

Zoe continued pounding on the door until someone propped it open, pushing her to the floor with an undignified thump. Zoe glared accusingly at Katrina, scrunched up her face, and started to cry.

"There, there." Mrs. Porter hurried into the room, scooped Zoe into her arms, and ten seconds later had her seated at the table with a handful of crayons and a whole stack of papers to demolish.

Katrina stood up so she wouldn't appear quite as lazy. She patted Brielle's head absently while the baby ripped the pages out of a picture book.

"Good morning, dear." Mrs. Porter pouted and stared over the top of her glasses. "I thought you were sick."

Katrina blushed under the scrutiny. "No, I ... Well, I didn't feel well when I woke up but ... It's my turn in the nursery. I mean I switched weeks since ..."

Mrs. Porter frowned and traded Brielle's ripped book for

a cloth one. "PG called me just before service. Said you weren't feeling well and asked if I could cover for you."

Katrina couldn't speak or sing in front of a crowd if her life depended on it, but she could play her violin without the slightest hint of stage fright. She did her best to draw from that same source of confidence to flash a convincing smile. "I must have miscommunicated with him. I'm sorry. I told him I would be ok down here, but he probably …"

Mrs. Porter was staring over her glasses again, pouting as if she had just thrown a lemon quarter in her mouth, peel and all. "Are you having …" She glanced ostentatiously at Katrina's midsection, and the hint of a smile cracked through her usually stern face. "Is this morning sickness, dear?"

Katrina's breath rushed out in a series of giggles that made her sound as silly as those high-school freshmen in Greg's youth group so many years ago. "No, no. Nothing like that."

A raised eyebrow. An unconvinced tilt of the head. "Really? Because I've been meaning to ask you ever since the women's retreat back in September when your appetite was so poor."

Katrina bit her lip. Stared at baby Brielle so contentedly eating the tag from the cloth book. Wished it were possible to disappear by sheer force of will. "It's nothing like that."

Mrs. Porter made a grumpy sound in the back of her throat. "Well, I had to ask. I remember one breakfast you got up to use the ladies' room twice, so it got some of us wondering, that's all."

"Thanks for being concerned." Katrina twisted her ring around her finger and glanced at the clock by the door. Might God have miraculously sped up the morning service to spare her this horrific encounter?

Mrs. Porter smacked her lips together. "Some of us were talking, you know. Wondering if you and PG were planning to get right down to business starting your family or piddle around and wait a few years like so many young folks do these days. And we hardly knew you back then, so none of us felt comfortable asking. But now that the subject's broached, when exactly do you and PG plan to make a kid?"

Katrina swallowed, hoping the ever-observant Mrs. Porter wouldn't notice the way her hands trembled. "We've decided to trust God's timing for that."

A haughty snort. Chin jerked upwards, sending her long Christmas tree earrings dangling. "If that's your philosophy, it's a wonder you're not halfway through your second trimester by now! What month was it that you got married?"

Katrina bit her lip while Mrs. Porter chortled.

"I'm sorry." She frowned. "I sometimes forget you're

new here and aren't completely used to me yet." She rubbed Katrina's shoulder. "I say what's on my mind, dear, but it's only because I care. A few of the ladies and I were talking about it, that's all. Saying how we'd love to see PG settle down with a baby or two of his own. And you." She stepped back and gave an apologetic half-smile. "You're such a tiny little wisp of a thing. Hardly more than a baby yourself. And there's nothing like carrying a child of your own to turn you into a real woman, that's all." Another uninvited back rub. "Well, I can see I've embarrassed you, and I'm awfully sorry for that. We'll get used to each other before long, I promise. In the meantime, you just ignore everything I've said, all right?"

She unwrapped a crayon that was giving Zoe a hard time.

"Well, sounds like the kids are calm here, so I'll leave you be."

Katrina held her breath, making a valiant effort to keep silent until Mrs. Porter left.

"Oh, speaking of kids." Mrs. Porter paused in the doorway and turned around. "Did PG talk to you about the Christmas pageant?"

"The what?"

"He was supposed to tell you last week. We always have a Christmas pageant. Nothing fancy, especially since we don't have as many children coming here these days. I don't know what it is about these young families refusing to raise their kids up properly. It's a real shame if you ask me. But anyway, what was I saying?" She strummed the doorknob with long, artificial fingernails that would have given any one of Katrina's violin teachers apoplexy. "That's right, the pageant. We always do some sort of musical. I figure with your background, it'll be a piece of cake. Well, you stay after church today, and I'll show you where the costumes are. I already told PG to put it in the bulletin that practices will start this Wednesday night. That way, I figured you could be down here to rehearse with the kids while PG does youth group upstairs. And if you need any more helpers, I told PG to find you a teen or two. They know what they're doing."

Brielle toddled to Mrs. Porter and tugged at her skirt. Mrs. Porter picked her up and plopped her into Katrina's arms. "Well, if you don't have any other questions for me, I'll just go upstairs and hear whatever's left of PG's sermon."

Brielle fussed and fidgeted in Katrina's hold. By the time Mrs. Porter had shut the door, Katrina and she were plunked down together in the rocker, one hollering loudly, the other stifling silent sobs.

CHAPTER 8

Katrina sat on the side of her bed, thankful the service was over. She didn't have time for cramps. Not this close to Christmas. Not with a pageant to plan, a pageant she hadn't even known about until Mrs. Porter marched in and put her in charge. What was Greg thinking? She was a second violinist, not a director. Not a leader. Who with half a brain would pick a girl who's too afraid to speak in public and can't even sing to direct a musical? Besides, she didn't know anything about kids. She had grown up an only child and had spent more time with her violin teachers than with children her own age. Every minute of her childhood that wasn't tied up with homework was spent practicing. Rehearsing. Performing. It was the only life she had known.

Until Greg.

She had always assumed she'd fall in love with someone in the orchestra. She adored the sound of the French horn and used to picture arriving to practice together with her husband. Spending their evenings together at rehearsals.

Sharing a music studio, with her teaching her violin and him teaching horn the next room over. Meeting a guitar-strumming youth pastor had never been part of the plan.

That was at least one thing she and her mother agreed on.

A pageant. Great. Just one more obligation. She still hadn't started any of her Christmas shopping. The budget was tighter than normal after so many unexpected medical bills. The church elders spoke vaguely of a Christmas bonus, but whether or not that would materialize in time to be of any use for the holidays was still a mystery. Katrina asked Greg to guess how much they'd have to work with, but he couldn't tell her. For all she knew, their bonus would be a McDonald's gift card and a copy of the utility bill with a handwritten note asking them to conserve more energy. So here they were, just a few weeks before Christmas, with enough outstanding medical bills to last them two more tax returns and no realistic way to buy each other presents.

Meanwhile, her mom was expecting the same kind of fancy gifts Katrina had purchased for her year after year, ever since she took her first violin teaching job in high school. Greg had mentioned Black Friday shopping in one of his most recent sermons, talking about how pointless it was to spend money you didn't have in order to buy things for people you didn't like. Well, it was all fine and good to look at it that way. Unless it was your own mother you were talking about. Then things got a little more complicated. Greg wanted to send Katrina's mom a gift card and forget about it, but it's hard to buy a gift card when every extra penny is paying off emergency room fees. Besides, something like that would only solidify her mom's conviction that Katrina had doomed herself to a life of poverty and squalor when she married Greg.

She changed out of her black dress and put on some loose-fitting sweat pants. At least Greg hadn't invited anyone over for lunch after church.

Had he?

She wracked her brain, trying to remember him saying anything about guests. If someone was coming over, he would have reminded her, right? He had seen how messy the house was when they left. He would have mentioned something, wouldn't he?

There was no real way to know for sure, not until he showed up with congregants in tow or not. She should probably tidy things up just to be safe, but she was exhausted. After Mrs. Porter left the nursery, Brielle had cried for half an hour until she finally fell asleep, drooling against Katrina's shoulder. It was a good thing Greg hadn't preached late or Katrina might have dozed on the job as well.

Stupid nursery. Why had she volunteered to work today anyway? Why had Greg let her? Didn't he know how hard it was for her after everything they had gone through? She thought about Joy Holmes, raising a hyperactive boy, two tiny girls, and now burdened with yet another pregnancy. Did she know how lucky she was? Did she know how some people would die to trade places with her, nauseated and fatigued as she might be?

Katrina sank her head on her pillow. Greg wouldn't come home until everybody else left the church. It could take half an hour from the time the sermon ended. Sometimes longer, especially if any of the elders had *constructive feedback* to impart. She really should get up and clean.

There was always too much to do. Katrina couldn't figure out how wives who worked full-time jobs of their own managed to get anything done around the house. Six months into marriage and she still couldn't keep up with the most basic of tasks. She had been managing all right until the fall ...

Why did everything have to come back to that? When would the memories stop haunting her? It would be one thing if Greg understood, but even though he had held her hand and taken care of her those first few days, as soon as he returned to work everything went back to normal. Could he really forget so quickly? Could he really bounce back to work as if nothing had happened? Greg didn't talk about it anymore. The sad thing was if Katrina were back in Long Beach, she'd find more sympathy from her orchestra friends than she did from her own husband.

All she really wanted was to plug in the heating pad and take a long nap. She had been so naïve last summer. She waltzed into marriage assuming Sunday afternoons would be the most relaxing part of the week, the Friday-night equivalent for a pastor's family. She envisioned lunches out at different restaurants. An afternoon enjoying a movie together or cuddling in bed. Even if Greg had work to do, she had pictured the two of them sitting on the couch, him with his studies, her with her journal. If it wouldn't distract him too much, she could practice her violin while he planned out his sermons.

God, what happened?

She sighed and thought about her violin. Dmitry Leonardo Cantarella, *Dmitry* after Shostakovich, her favorite composer and *Leonardo Cantarella* after the violin maker. Greg couldn't understand why she would name her violin or refer to him as a *he*. Until he teased her about it, she hadn't even stopped to wonder if that kind of behavior was normal. Didn't the other violinists in the orchestra name their instruments as well? She had never thought to ask.

She glanced at her zipped-up case. Maybe she should take him out. She'd never neglected him for so long before. She still wet the humidifier each day so the wood wouldn't crack, especially in this deplorably dry and chilly winter weather. Greg laughed whenever he saw her *water* her violin. But even though she kept that routine up religiously, she hadn't played him in almost two months. She missed the feel of her jaw against his chin rest, the weight of the bow perfectly balanced in her hand. Her ears longed for his sweet, lyrical tone. Maybe she'd take him out this afternoon. Maybe today was the day she'd find the courage ...

The front door opened. Good. Greg was home. They could have a quick lunch, and then she might practice some. Get her mind off church politics and utility bills and Christmas pageants and hospital fees.

"Hi, babe," Greg called out. His voice was cheerful. That must mean he went a full Sunday with no rude comments from disgruntled parishioners. No awkward meetings with elders who took it upon themselves to point out how everything her husband was doing at Orchard Grove Bible Church was wrong.

She swept her hair out of her eyes and smiled. She needed more Tylenol, but at least her cramps weren't as bad as they'd been this morning. She headed down the hall.

Greg stood in the entryway with Nancy Higgins, the church treasurer, and her husband. At first, Katrina was so appalled at the piles of unfolded laundry on the couch and the two full trash bags by the front door that she forgot about her own appearance.

"So you changed into something comfortable," Nancy exclaimed, eyeing the faded sweat pants. "Good for you."

Katrina searched Nancy's tone for a hint of sarcasm and flushed. "I'm sorry. I just …" She picked up the trash bags and tossed them into the laundry room along with her bathrobe. She grabbed a basket to hold the extra clothes.

"Don't worry about tidying up on our account," Nancy called after her. "We're just here for the food, not the view."

Katrina froze, trying to decide if she should be mad at herself for forgetting or at Greg for not telling her to expect company. There were too many other things to do to worry about it for long. She dumped the laundry basket aside and hurried to the kitchen, wincing through the pain. She opened the fridge, praying to find something easy she could throw together for lunch.

God, what's happening?

CHAPTER 9

"Well, Katrina, you certainly do know how to put a mind at ease." Nancy crossed her arms and sat back in her chair. "I feel right at home here."

Katrina glanced surreptitiously at the living room. The piles of laundry. The scattered books. More sarcasm, maybe?

"I'm sorry lunch wasn't fancier." She eyed the cold sandwiches on her company's plates.

Nancy shook her head and wiped her mouth with a paper towel.

"It was delicious. Don't worry about a thing. Back when I was expecting, I was lucky if I could work a can opener." She chuckled but froze when she saw Katrina's face.

"I'm sorry. Were you waiting to tell people?"

Another cramp. She didn't look at Greg. Didn't trust herself to keep her composure. She felt her husband's hand on her lap but didn't return his gentle squeeze.

"Oh, dear." Nancy looked around the table imploringly.

"I thought ... The way you kept using the bathroom at the ladies retreat, I just assumed ... I'm terribly sorry." She fidgeted with her paper towel. "What a mess I've made. If it helps, you never did look it. I said just a week or two ago that you're still as petite as ever. Not showing at all." Her eyes flitted from person to person. She let out a nervous laugh. "See what happens when we start speculating? I assure you I'm mortified. Here I was thinking ..."

"Katrina had a miscarriage in October." Greg's voice was soft. Barely audible over Nancy's nervous laugh.

Every eye bored into Katrina's face. Burning hot. She felt her body diminish. Could she squeeze herself into a little speck? A staccato dot? Could she disappear?

Nancy and her husband sat frozen in their chairs. Katrina focused on the laundry in the next room. She was the most pathetic pastor's wife in the history of Orchard Grove Bible Church. Couldn't clean house. Couldn't cook. Couldn't entertain without wanting to run from the table in tears.

Bejeweled fingers gripping her hand. Sympathetic gazes crushing down on her until she grew smaller. A dot. Invisible.

"I'm so sorry, honey." Whispered words unable to pierce the protective armor erected around her heart. Mumbled phrases that wounded rather than healed. "I had no idea."

"I'd like to be excused." The voice wasn't her own. It

was small. Scared. Like a mouse. Her legs carried her away from the table. Down the hall. She ran her finger along the wall to keep from stumbling.

Once in her room, she shut the door. She wasn't crying. Not yet. Her legs shook as she knelt by her bed. Her fingers trembled as she unzipped the case.

Dmitry Leonardo Cantarella. Her instrument. Her baby.

She left the bow untouched. He didn't make a sound. She wrapped her arms around her violin, inhaled the familiar vapors from his polish. Careful not to wet the wood, she held him close to her chest until her tears ran dry.

CHAPTER 10

"You awake, Mouse?" Greg's voice was tentative as he propped open their bedroom door.

Katrina roused herself from her half stupor and muttered something.

"Can I come in?" he asked.

She responded with another mumble, which he must have taken to mean yes.

He sat on the edge of her bed and felt her forehead just like her mother used to do when she was sick. "You ok?"

She wasn't mad at him. She wasn't even mad at Nancy Higgins and her invasive assumptions. Nancy was right. Katrina should be well into the second trimester by now. Should be showing. Maybe if she was lucky she'd be experiencing that pregnancy glow women talked about. Not lying in bed with cramps almost as painful as the miscarriage itself.

A little baby. A tiny, precious life. What went wrong? Why had God taken him away from her? She'd never know the baby's real gender, but secretly she had named him Peter. Strong. Mischievous, even. Like *Peter and the Wolf.*

"Nancy called," Greg was saying. "She asked me to apologize again."

Katrina didn't reply.

"She told me she had a miscarriage, too. Sounds a lot like what you went through. End of the first trimester. No reason for it, at least not that the doctors could explain. She said the same thing the nurse told us, remember? There was probably something wrong developmentally."

Would he ever stop talking? Didn't he understand? Didn't any of them understand? Her miscarriage wasn't *Mother Nature's way* to keep a sick kid from living. Didn't they get it? Greg, of all people — didn't he understand she'd rather have a disabled child than a dead one?

He had gotten over the entire ordeal so quickly. Did he even think about their child anymore? Their baby?

Peter.

Greg was frowning at her. Still stroking her forehead. "Maybe you should call her. It might be helpful to talk to someone who's gone through something like this before."

As if Greg hadn't gone through it with her. At least, he should have. She had been practicing her violin that horrific Tuesday night when the first stitching pain stung her side.

Half an hour later, the bleeding started. She called Greg into the bathroom. "What do you want me to do?" he asked.

A couple hours later, after going through several pads and holding two frantic conversations with the after-hours phone nurse, they hurried to the emergency room. He held her hand. Prayed with her in the car. After the doctor told them the ultrasound didn't show a heartbeat, they had cried together. Asked God why he would take their precious child. A child they would never name. A child Katrina could never hold.

Why, God?

The nurse handed her heavy-duty pads and told her what to expect. At least, Katrina thought she had. The nurse hadn't mentioned how severe the cramping would be. How Katrina would sit on the toilet, watching it fill up with blood. How every five minutes her husband would ask her if she thought they should go back to the ER.

No, the nurse hadn't prepared her at all. *Moderate to severe cramping. Bleeding like a heavy period.* If that was a heavy period, Katrina wondered how any woman could survive her monthly menses.

That night, they slept curled up together even though Greg usually hated if even their feet touched in the night. The next morning, he took off work and hardly let her get out of bed. They read together for the first time since moving to Washington. They were on *Voyage of the Dawn Treader* now. He insisted on doing all the reading and nearly made it to the last chapter.

And then, after a two-day convalescence, Katrina said she was feeling better. Said she'd like to get out of bed for a bit. The bleeding had slowed down by then, and she was sick of being cooped up with her depressing thoughts. She suggested it might be nice to get out of town for a day or two. See something outside of Orchard Grove. Weren't the apple orchards supposed to be busy in the fall? Maybe there was a tour they could take together. Taste fresh apple cider. Pick a basket to take home. Anything to take her mind off what had happened.

But Greg had missed two and a half days of work already. He couldn't afford any more time off. He never said so, but Katrina wondered if he was glad she had miscarried on a Tuesday so he could still work on his sermon before Sunday rolled around. The apple orchards would have to wait.

And so would Katrina. Greg must have thought that her saying she was feeling a little better meant she was perfectly healed. So he shut himself in his office at the church, working extra hours to make up for lost time. And Katrina waited. Waited for her body to return to some semblance of normalcy. Waited for her heart to stop aching. Waited for her soul to believe that all things — even this miscarriage — could work out for something good.

And in the meantime, she hadn't played her violin. How could she?

"So, what do you think?"

She had missed the flow of their one-sided conversation. "Think about what?"

A sigh, but at least not an angry one. "I said, how would you feel about going out to The Creamery for a treat?"

"Ice cream? In the middle of winter?"

He nodded. Smiling. Would their son have inherited that same grin? Would he have one day won the heart of a young teenage girl, scared to venture off on her own, scared to follow the man she loved?

Her stomach rumbled. Her husband looked down at her expectantly. Hopefully.

Her Greg.

"You don't want to, do you?"

"I'm sorry. I still don't feel well."

He pursed his lips together. "I thought you might say that." The same smile. "So I brought a back-up plan." He pulled a book out from under his arm. "Is this better?"

Voyage of the Dawn Treader. She looked at the clock. Nearly four. Another hour before she'd have to think about dinner. Two hours before they'd head back to church for the monthly business meeting. She winced as she sat up in bed. Greg situated himself next to her and opened the book. "Ready?" he asked.

"Sure," she said and leaned her head against his chest, letting his voice rise and fall over the ocean of pain in her aching soul.

CHAPTER 11

She needed to play. Needed to feel her violin strings against her fingers, needed to press her jaw against her chin rest, her ear so close to that freshly polished wood. Close enough to feel every vibration, close enough for the music to seep into her core. To warm and soothe her soul.

How had she ignored him for so long?

Her Dmitry.

Greg was next door at the business meeting. He had insisted she stay home, and she surprised herself by agreeing without a fight. She hadn't washed any of the dishes from dinner yet. The living room was just as cluttered as it appeared during Nancy Higgins' surprise visit, but none of that mattered.

She just needed her music.

She plucked the strings. Even with the change in weather, Dmitry was surprisingly in tune for having been neglected for two months. No, not neglected. Katrina had rinsed his humidifier every day. Polished his wood at least once a week, whenever she needed to feel the comforting smoothness of his skin. She had feared at one point that her violin would be mad at her. Greg would tease her, of course, if he knew the extent to which she personified her instrument. But some things her chord-strumming husband would never understand. There existed parts of her soul where Greg's hands couldn't touch. His caress couldn't warm. His love couldn't reach.

There were dark places. Primitive, dangerous places, yet capable of so much beauty.

So much awe.

She tightened her bow.

She was ready.

She wondered if her friends from the symphony ever associated different music with smells. She often did. There was the scent of her high-school orchestra room just across from the gym. A mix of chalk, sweat, and a hint of chlorine from the nearby pool. The practice room for the Long Beach Symphony was different. Rosin. Perfume. A whiff of cigarette smoke wafting over from Stan's collar beside her.

But as she held her violin now, she could only smell the antiseptic scent of the emergency room. Alcohol swabs. Laundry soap. Bleached linens. Would she ever forget?

The acoustics in her bedroom were far from ideal. When they first moved into the parsonage, she had spent an entire afternoon hunting for the best practice spot. Her first choice would have been the room Greg claimed as his office. More often than not she ended up playing in the kitchen, which gave her music a bright, open ring. But if she was sad, if she was nursing a bruised ego after yet another run-in with Mrs. Porter or any other member of the Women's Missionary League, Katrina preferred to play in her bedroom where the curtains and carpet, the pillows and blankets on the bed absorbed so much of the sound, making it mellow. Heavy. Somber.

She could pull off bright and airy when the score called for it, but Dmitry excelled in the lower tones. Her teacher once joked that Katrina's violin must have been a cello in a former life. No matter how much searching she did on the internet, Katrina couldn't find out much about Leonardo Cantarella, the Italian craftsman who delivered her instrument into the world, but she imagined his life must have been filled with both suffering and beauty. The pain and longing for redemption seeped into the very wood of her violin.

So beautiful.

So heart-wrenching.

She brought Dmitry to her shoulder and shut her eyes. She loved the feel of her bow in her hand, perfectly weighted, balancing her soul in a way she could never express in words. There were some things beyond language. Things that could only be spoken through music.

She let her bow caress the open string. A low, resonant sound. She didn't need vibrato. The instrument did that for her. Pulses of love. Waves of beauty.

Her violin.

Tentatively, she let her fingers meander up the board. The melody was slow. Hypnotic. She had composed a song for Greg just before they got engaged. She was so excited to play it for him, so eager to express her fears, her hopes, her love. But he couldn't understand. She left his apartment that night feeling lost. Lonely.

Tonight, her rhythm was lilting. Like lovers stalling in the morning. Reminding her of those places in her soul where Greg could never venture. Places he would never see. Never know.

Lonely places.

Her notes were higher now. A dance of sorts, herself and her violin. At times like these, she was certain she could be happy alone. Perfectly alone. Just herself. Her music. Her Dmitry.

Faster now. A chase. Groping for that perfect run, that perfect phrase. Coming so close to the realization, always falling just a bow hair short of achievement. Her music was beautiful. Haunting in its drive toward even greater perfection. She had spent a decade and a half seeking that sublime moment her teachers spoke of. That elusive paradise, sometimes lasting only a few fleeting seconds. Seconds in which your music is so true, so clear, so glorious you know you could never repeat your performance, not even after a lifetime of practice.

She had come close. Oh, she had come close. On more than one occasion. And yet her soul ached for a beauty she feared she would never realize this side of heaven. She played on. Let the music swell inside her. Anoint her. Sometimes it was hard to know whether to compare it to drowning or paradise. During her engagement, she wondered if intimacy with her husband would be similar.

She focused on her music. Beauty. Chilling in its acute rawness. Intensity. Passion. Longing. Like a prayer. Like being bathed with the Holy Spirit.

Her music and no one else's. Powerful. Primitive. Rhythm that would hold you in its caress, never relenting until it left you breathless.

A stitch in her side. Mom always told her she looked silly rocking back and forth like that while she played. Almost as pathetic as when she tried to sing.

A zinging pain like the day she lost her baby. Those cramps again.

She put down her bow.

Her song was done.

CHAPTER 12

"You're still in bed?"

She glanced at the clock before looking at her husband. Almost nine. Orchard Grove Bible could never run a business meeting in less than two and a half hours.

She sat up and adjusted the blankets around her. "How did everything go?"

"Oh, fine," Greg huffed and loosened his collar.

"Anything important come up?" she asked out of habit, certain she didn't want to know.

"Everything's important at those meetings. You know how riled up people get."

She searched his face for signs of strain. Was she making him even more stressed out? When they were engaged, she pictured herself creating a calm, peaceful home where he could relax after work. She imagined long talks far into the night. Drives through apple country. Leisurely walks around the neighborhood.

Her mom was right about one thing. Katrina had no idea

what she was getting into when she and Greg said *I do.*

"How was your night here?"

Katrina searched his voice for that familiar accusatory tone. The same tone he'd use after he'd emerge from his office at the church, glance at the messy dishes, the loads of laundry dumped on the couch and ask, "What was your day like?" A question which could be so innocuous if it weren't for that particular upturn of his eyebrows. The tell-tale tilt of his head.

She couldn't figure him out sometimes. "I'm all right," she answered.

"Yeah? How are those cramps?"

"Better."

She used to love watching him perform the most mundane tasks. Slipping out of his work clothes. Stretching his muscles before climbing into bed beside her.

"Oh, we talked about the pageant tonight. I guess Mrs. Porter mentioned it to you today in the nursery?"

They were both lying on their backs. Katrina stared at the ceiling, at the tiny cottage-cheese bumps that made constellations overhead. "Yeah." She was only paying half attention. In those intricate snowflake-like designs above her were notes. Music she could play if only she could hear it a little more clearly. Music she could touch if she could quiet her soul long enough. She pressed her fingers into her palm, playing on an imaginary fingerboard.

"If you want, I can see about finding a teen or two to help out at rehearsals."

She didn't want to talk about that. Didn't want to focus on anything but the sound she was making in her mind. Before she married Greg, she had been so free with her music. She could make her violin mimic her emotions with the draw of a bow. She could put fire and longing into her instrument and then turn around and perform the exact same strain with a haunting sadness that could leave her listeners chilled.

Now her music was chaotic. Disorganized. Even when she played at church before the miscarriage, the notes had been rote. Scripted for her by someone else's hand. Would she ever play like herself again?

She had only practiced five or ten minutes tonight. Her side still smarted.

She tightened the blankets around her. Shut her eyes. Imagined how Dmitry felt inside his weather-proof, velvet-lined case. Did he enjoy the solitude? Did his strings still echo with the last refrains she played?

Greg was saying something about budget cuts for the holiday dinners the church passed out each year. She was glad he didn't mention the icy sidewalks or the neglected light downstairs. Before long he was mumbling. She couldn't imagine putting her voice through what he did every Sunday. She couldn't imagine speaking in public either, so it was a good thing she was just the pastor's wife.

Pastor's wife. The title had sounded so important. Glamorous even as she had prepared to marry the pastor-elect of Orchard Grove Bible Church. Nobody had warned her about the endless calls to nursery volunteers, the lunch and dinner guests once or twice a week who seemed eager to comment on Katrina's obvious lack of experience in the kitchen, the impossible expectations of Mrs. Porter and the entire Women's Missionary League.

"… will both be out of town, so we'll need someone to help lead worship the Sunday before Christmas. I said between the two of us we'd work it out."

She stopped fingering along with her imaginary music. "What?"

"Well, I figured with my guitar and your violin, we could pull something together."

"You told them that?" Her pitch rose against her will. That was another mistake she had made during her engagement. She assumed pastors' wives didn't raise their voices.

He was staring at the ceiling too. Was he watching the patterns? Listening for their song?

She twisted her ring around her finger. "You know I can't sing."

"Nobody's asking you to. Just play along with me while everyone else sings. No big deal."

Her heart raced higher into her chest until she feared it might leap into her throat and gag her. Her ribcage squeezed in to about half its usual size. She couldn't take in a deep breath. "I can't believe you told them I'd play."

"You used to play every Sunday."

"That was for accompaniment. What do you think I can do, just plunk out the melody while everyone sings along?"

He inhaled deeply. She envied his lungs. "I hadn't thought that far, to be honest. All I thought was I'm married to a first-class violinist, she's agreed to play in church before, this time we'll just be short a few singers. No big deal."

Her mind threw out so many counter arguments she didn't know which to scream at him first. She lay still, frozen in her fortress of blankets. There were no musical patterns in the ceiling now, only a storm, a blizzard.

Greg rolled onto his side to face her. "Talk to me, Mouse. What are you thinking?"

Where should she start? She was thinking about how the last time she had played her violin — really played it, not tinkered around for a few minutes — her child had died. She was thinking about how many times during the interview process both she and Greg had informed everyone that she was not a worship leader. She was thinking about why Greg would volunteer her when he knew how traumatic it was for her to have to play any time she felt pressured into it.

What was she thinking? There were too many ways to answer the question, all of them resulting in more arguments. "Nothing," she answered.

"So you'll do it?"

Why was he pushing?

"Fine." Isn't that what a pastor's wife was supposed to say? Support her husband in his ministry. Put his needs before her own. Even the church's needs if it came to it. But that was the thing. He didn't need her. Couldn't he get up and strum his guitar and lead worship on his own? What purpose would it serve having her up there unless it was to appease those meddling members of the Women's Missionary League who were just *dying* to hear her play again? Isn't that what this really came down to? She envisioned events as they must have unfolded at the business meeting. The two other vocalists mentioned they'd be out of town a particular Sunday. Greg said he could lead with his guitar. And then someone, Mrs. Porter or one of her many busybody clones, would have said something like, "Oh, and you should ask Katrina to lead worship with you. You know, we've missed her violin so much since she quit playing all of a sudden."

Katrina had been to enough of those monthly business meetings to picture everything, right down to the nods of the less vocal members of the League who might not have voiced the same suggestion but supported it all the same.

This is what she got from Greg. Her husband. The man who was supposed to know her better than anyone else in the world. The man who was supposed to protect her. Love her sacrificially. Not use her like some pulpit prop to make his own preaching career more successful.

"You shaking, Mouse?"

"It's just cold in here." She knew better than to expect him to offer to turn up the thermostat.

"You ready for me to turn off the light?"

She rolled over and faced the wall. "Yeah."

"Good night."

No, it wasn't a good night. But it could have been worse. She let out a choppy breath, glad her lungs had decided to function a little better than before. Greg's phone beeped, and she wondered for a fleeting moment who would be texting him after nine. His phone's glow cast a blue light on the wall as he checked his message.

"Good night," she whispered, doubting he even heard.

CHAPTER 13

"I thought you said you'd just play melody during the chorus." Greg rested his forearm against the side of his guitar.

Katrina tried to meet his glare. Over the past half an hour in the sanctuary, she had practiced her exit speech a dozen times. This wasn't working. She couldn't do it. He had to realize that. Instead, she just mumbled, "Sorry."

He placed his pick on the music stand. "Look, if you don't want to do this, just say so. It'll go faster if I practice by myself anyway."

She knew he didn't mean what he said. He was offering her an out, but if she took it, he'd make her regret it. A subtle jab, a sideways glance, somehow she'd have to pay. She closed her eyes. Felt the bow between her fingers. Could she ever find that balance she was looking for?

"So are you doing melody or what?"

She didn't know how to answer him. She was a second violinist. Harmonies made her music rich and vibrant. How was there any room for creative expression in plunking out the notes to a simple worship chorus? Besides, the congregation would be singing the melody. Why did they need her playing the exact same tune?

Why did they need her playing at all?

She wiped her hands on her pants legs. Nothing Dmitry hated more than a sweaty fingerboard.

"All right," Greg said, "should we go from the bridge?"

Katrina raised her violin to her shoulder. Why did these modern songwriters insist on throwing in bridges? It was ridiculous, the musical equivalent of filling up an entire chapter of a novel with the same monotonous sentence over and over and over, maybe switching around the words every third or fourth line. But she was just whining now. She gave Greg a nod. She was ready.

Her playing was rusty. Twice she had missed a run she could hear perfectly in her head but her fingers couldn't keep up with her brain. She should have never taken those two months off practicing.

Then again, she should have never agreed to play with Greg in the first place.

"What's wrong now?" Greg asked when she tucked her violin under her arm in the middle of the piece.

"That's supposed to be a D7," she said. "You've been playing a D."

Greg pouted and bent over his music stand. "Ok, you're right. Not that it's a huge difference."

"Yeah, it is huge. That's why it always sounds so awkward when we lead into the chorus."

He penciled something onto his sheet of music. "Sounded all right to me."

"I'm sure it did," she mumbled.

"What?"

"Never mind." She brought her violin up to her shoulder again. "Can we just start over, go through the whole thing, and be done with it?"

He threw his pencil onto the music stand. It bounced off the metal lip and landed on the floor. "Great." He crouched down, still balancing his guitar on his lap. "Did you see where it went?" His tone was brusque. Accusatory.

"How should I know?"

"I never said you should know. I just asked if you did know."

She frowned. During her engagement, she had daydreamed about this very thing, playing her violin while Greg piddled around on his guitar. It wasn't a symphonic arrangement, but at least they could make music together. But whenever they tried in reality, she could barely stand the sound of his tinny, made-in-China hunk of wood with strings. He wasn't even in sync with his instrument enough to know when he went flat.

"Here it is." Greg picked up the pencil and replaced it on its stand. "All right. You ready to play now?"

"Fine."

He strummed the intro. She had known even before they began dating he couldn't maintain a steady tempo, so she didn't bother to correct him when he sped up halfway into the first verse.

Majestic love, come fill me with your songs.

Almighty God, forgive me all my wrongs.

The music was supposed to make her feel repentant. Not that she needed that reminder. She knew how many times she had blown it. How many times she had let her temper flare up and get between her and Greg. But she wasn't the only one. Their first night in the parsonage, he had yelled at her for taking too long to wash her hair. As if an extra three or four minutes running the hot water would blow the church budget.

A week later, he asked her why the flower beds in the front yard were covered in weeds. Here she was, with half their belongings still packed in boxes, and he was worried about flowers she hadn't even planted? "They expect us to keep up the house and yard." It was a phrase she had already grown sick of after seven long days in the parsonage.

Sometimes she daydreamed about getting her own job so they could afford to rent a place of their own.

Burning fire, your love consumes my soul.

Savior God, your mercy makes me whole.

She had been so naïve to think Greg could ever complete her. They weren't partners, working in harmony like a violin and a bow. They were more like a snare drum without a stick and a single cymbal. Technically they could make sound, but it certainly wasn't music.

Gracious Father, cover all my sin.

Perfect love, revive my heart again.

A simple verse. A pretty enough melody if you were into modern worship songs. The problem was that the members of Orchard Grove Bible Church had grown up on hymns, gotten married with hymns, raised their children with hymns, and buried their beloved departed to the tune of even more hymns. No one knew what to do with a young youth pastor from southern California rushing in and assaulting the status quo with his guitar and pick.

Katrina was sick of the bickering. There wasn't a single business meeting yet where the music issue hadn't been thoroughly argued. Did it really matter what year a song was written if it glorified God? She had to admit she liked a lot of hymns for their musical and aesthetic qualities, but the words could be so convoluted or even flat-out ridiculous.

On the other hand, lyrics from the modern stuff could be just as awkward and immature. And if the songwriter didn't have anything else to add, he just tacked on a bridge or repeated the last line of the chorus a dozen times or so to make sure the words sank in.

Heavenly peace, flood me.

Heavenly peace, flood me.

Your face is all I seek.

Heavenly peace, flood me.

Greg stopped strumming halfway through the drawn-out repetition. "Mouse, you look like you hate the world. Do you want to be done?"

She played one more line before she stopped. "Whatever."

"No, it's not *whatever*. I'm really worried about you. If you don't want to be here, why don't you go home?"

She gritted her teeth. "I'm fine." She hated this song more than a lot of the others Greg chose. It felt as if she had been working on it with him for hours. Why couldn't they wrap up rehearsal, lock up the church, and call it a night?

Greg set his pick down. "You definitely don't look fine."

What did he want? For her to admit how miserable she was?

"Can we just get to the end and then go home?" She kept her violin against her chin.

"No. I want to know what's going on. Are you mad because I asked you to play?"

Her palms were sweaty again. "It's not that."

"I think it is. You've been angry with me ever since I asked you to fill in. If you didn't want to do it, why didn't you say so last week when it first came up?"

She poised her bow on the string. "I just want to finish this song."

"Not until you tell me why you're mad."

"I'm not mad!" Why wouldn't he ever believe her?

"Anything you say." He stepped down from the stage. "I don't feel like practicing anymore. I'm going home." He paused to look over his shoulder when he was halfway out of the sanctuary. "You coming?"

"Pretty soon." She made a show of flipping through her pages on the music stand even though she could play all of Greg's little church ditties without the aid of song sheets.

"Whatever," he mumbled. "Turn the lights out when you're done."

As if she could have forgotten.

CHAPTER 14

Her violin days were over. That's all there was to it. She'd never play again, not like she used to. Her mom had warned her before she moved to Orchard Grove. "You'll grow rusty without your lessons and your symphony."

Katrina hadn't believed her and like a baby had blindly followed her husband to this desert wasteland, where even the apple trees knew better than to grow in the middle of such an ugly, miserable town. The summer heat was oppressive, worse than anything she had experienced in Long Beach. Of course, the parsonage didn't have an air conditioner, but even if it did, Greg would have refused to touch it. Heaven forbid they rack up an extra ten bucks on the church's utilities bill.

Then after a bleak autumn came an even bleaker winter. Katrina had been so excited to live in a state with occasional snow. She didn't know that every single dusting of white turned to mud within a day or two. The smog-stained skyline of Los Angeles was more appealing.

She hadn't played a single note on her violin since Greg stormed out of the sanctuary an hour earlier. She had thumbed through his song folder and was reminded again how stubborn he was for forcing contemporary choruses on a church as rigid and traditional as Orchard Grove Bible. Ditties like those had worked fine in Long Beach, but this was different. Different audience, different culture, different life.

Katrina thought of her symphony friends, wondered what pieces they were working on now. The string section had given her such a touching good-bye, taken her out for dessert at The Cheesecake Factory, tried to get her to drink a celebratory glass of wine in honor of her upcoming wedding. Nearly all of them had hugged her good-bye, and when she got to Orchard Grove there was a wedding card signed by all the violinists and half the other musicians waiting for her.

That had been a real family. Not the bickering, back-stabbing members of Orchard Grove Bible Church who could spend twenty minutes arguing about whether the new tablecloths should be put into the kitchen line-item of the budget or women's ministry. As if that had anything to do with saving the lost souls of north-central Washington.

She thought about the night ahead. Greg was probably angry. Would probably still be angry no matter what time she headed home. She hated living so close to the church. If they rented a place of their own, he could commute to work. How much trouble would that solve if they weren't constantly in each other's space? She had been keeping her eye on the Orchard Grove classifieds just in case a part-time job popped up.

It wasn't just the extra money that made the sound of work so appealing. It was time out of the home. Six months after the move, she still felt like a guest living in someone else's house. People felt free to stop by unannounced any time, night or day. Since the parsonage belonged to the church, that gave every single member of Orchard Grove the assumed role of landlord. Landlords who made their tenants salt their own frozen walkways and unclog their own drains.

Landlords who complained over every single utility bill.

But if she had a job of her own, she and Greg could at least cover utilities at the parsonage even if they didn't rent their own place. It didn't need to be much, nothing full time, just something to save her from the deplorable apple country boredom. She had looked into opening a violin studio, but the Orchard Grove public school system didn't even have a strings program, and she wasn't about to start with a classroom of first-timers and spend six months on *Twinkle, Twinkle*.

She twisted her wedding ring. Dinner would probably be

late. Another reason for Greg to be grumpy. He wouldn't say anything about it, not outright, but he would make a show of looking at his cell phone during the meal and declare something like, "Wow, where'd the evening go?"

She eyed her case. She felt like she had betrayed Dmitry by playing simple church ditties and then just holding him after Greg left. Her husband probably thought she was over here rehearsing his choruses. Oh well. At least it was an excuse to get out from underneath the same roof for a change.

She was halfway through tucking her violin in his case when she heard the door of the church open. "Pastor Greg? You here?"

Katrina glanced around, wondering if there was time to sneak behind the baptistery without being seen.

"Oh, hello, Katrina. Is that you?"

She glanced up, pretending to be startled. "Nancy. I didn't hear you come in." She hadn't seen the Higginses since that awful lunch on Sunday.

Nancy glanced around the sanctuary. "Do you come here to practice?"

Katrina flushed but couldn't have said why. "Sometimes. I mean, I was just getting a few things ready. For church."

Nancy had crossed her arms and was scrutinizing her. "Well, since we're here alone, I hope Pastor Greg passed on my phone message to you the other day. I just felt like you might want to know it's not uncommon what you went through. They say one out of four ..." Her voice trailed off.

Katrina had heard that statistic, too, but it didn't make sense. How did so many women pick up the pieces of their shattered dreams and go on living their normal, everyday lives?

"I'm still sorry to have stumbled onto the truth the way I did, but now that it's out in the open, I hope you'll be willing to talk about it if that would ever be helpful."

Katrina stared at her violin case. "Thank you."

"Well, I better be going." Nancy straightened her scarf, which Katrina recognized from one of her mom's fancy catalogs. "I only stopped by to drop off some canned food for the Christmas boxes." She gave a little nod. "You call me if you need anything, all right?" She looked around the sanctuary. "Nobody else's here, are they?"

Katrina shook her head.

"Good." She held out her car keys. "I'm going to prop open the back door until I've emptied the trunk. Don't tell anyone I'm wasting heat." She gave Katrina a conspiratorial wink. "I hear some people pitch a fit over the utility bills around here."

CHAPTER 15

"I'm sorry dinner was late." Katrina tried to break the silence with an apology. She and Greg hadn't exchanged more than half a dozen words since she came creeping home from the church with her violin case strapped across her chest.

Greg shrugged and took a bite of hamburger casserole.

"I saw Nancy earlier," Katrina said. "She was bringing over some food for the Christmas boxes."

"Good."

Katrina stared over Greg's shoulders. She hadn't finished the dishes from last night's dinner yet. There was always so much to do, even though she hardly felt busy. Some days would pass by, and she couldn't figure out what she'd done with herself. She knew there were enough hours to cover the basic things like dishes and laundry, but even if she had the time, she couldn't find the energy.

Or the will.

Things had gotten worse since she stopped playing

Dmitry regularly. What joy was there for her in a cold, dreary world devoid of harmony?

"You ok?" she finally asked tentatively. That was one of the worst parts about her fights with Greg. She never knew when they were over. She'd watch him for cues, but sometimes he'd stay cold and frigid for days. Other times he forgot about their arguments so quickly it left her head reeling.

Greg shrugged again. "Yeah. Just thinking about my sermon."

So he wasn't mad, then? Or he wasn't bothering to waste his mental energy on her right now? Well, if he was ready to move on, so was she.

"What are you preaching about this week?"

"A lot of different things. It's hard to explain."

"What verses are you using?"

He scooped another helping of hamburger helper onto his plate. "Several."

"I'm sorry I was in a grumpy mood earlier." She kept her eyes on his face to check for signs of confrontation. "I've been really tired."

He met her gaze a split second before she could glance away. "That's what I've been hearing for the last two months."

"It's just ..." No, this wasn't fair. She had apologized to him. Why was he bringing up the past? She hid her hands in her lap and fidgeted with her ring.

"Did you schedule your doctor appointment yet?"

Why was he doing this? Why was he changing the subject? "No."

The doctor asked her to come back in a few weeks after the miscarriage, but she didn't need another medical bill to worry about right before Christmas.

"So for all you know, you're anemic or there's some other problem and that's why you're so tired. Except we'll never figure it out because you never scheduled your follow-up at the clinic."

She played back the last few lines of their conversation. How had they gone from her apology about music practice to a fight over the doctor?

"It's not anemia." She was sure of that much at least. Greg couldn't eat a meal without meat. Her vegetarian mother would die of shock if she came up to Orchard Grove and scrutinized their meal plan. If there was anything wrong with Katrina's diet, it was that she wasn't getting enough fruit. Washington was just fine in the summer, but in the winter there was hardly anything to buy except for oranges and bananas. And of course apples.

Plenty of apples.

"I just worry about you, Mouse," Greg said with his mouth full. "You know that."

"Yeah, ok. I'll try to remember to call the doctor's tomorrow." She knew she would forget, but hopefully now they could at least move on.

Greg took a noisy gulp of lemonade. "By the way, I feel bad practice didn't go as well today. I've just had a lot on my mind."

She knew that much was true, at least. There hadn't been a single day since they arrived in Orchard Grove when Greg didn't have a lot on his mind. He could preach to his congregants about not worrying, but he was probably the most high-strung, stressed out person Katrina knew. If he could learn to relax every once in a while …

"I guess I had a different idea in mind when I said we'd lead worship." Greg set his elbows on the table. "I thought it would give us something to do together. Something we both enjoy."

Guilt rushed through and heated her gut.

"You've been so sad lately," he went on. "I hoped this would help pull you out of whatever funk you've been in. But I shouldn't have forced it on you if you weren't ready."

They were both staring down into their laps. *I forgive*

you. The words hung on the tip of her tongue, but she realized he had never actually said he was sorry. If she offered her forgiveness, would that just make things worse? Make him feel like she was blaming him?

It was her fault as much as his. She realized that now. He had been trying to help. You couldn't blame him for his motives, at least. But music was such a simple thing to Greg. He could play his guitar just as easily as not. When he wasn't practicing, he wasn't pining away for his instrument, wondering what masterpiece he'd create when they were together again. He could go weeks, probably months, without making music. Dreaming about music. Listening to music. Take away his guitar, and he was still Pastor Greg.

She wasn't like that. Back in Long Beach, if carpal tunnel made her slow down for a week or two, she was miserable. If she could only play one or two hours a day instead of the usual four or five, she felt empty, like a lonely, gaping chasm was waiting to suck her into its soundless void.

She had never gone a full two months without playing before. And Greg thought she could just pick up her instrument and accompany his little choruses for church like nothing happened? He didn't know. He'd never experienced the sizzling fear that consumed her gut when she realized she might never play in an orchestra again. He didn't understand the chaos that swarmed around in her mind as one silent day followed another. Like Beethoven trapped in a soundless world. Or Handel still trying to compose after a medical quack stole away his sight.

How did they do it? How did they keep from growing mad? Beethoven without his hearing was still arguably the greatest of the Romantic composers. Handel without his eyesight could still open the heavens and reveal God's glory in a way that no other mortal ever had or would. But Katrina without her music? What was she?

A pastor's wife, and a pathetic one at that. A reluctant nursery coordinator. A lousy cook. A deplorable housekeeper.

That was all.

"You know what this dinner needs?" Greg stood up from the table. "Some dessert."

Katrina mentally inventoried the cupboards. "I don't think we have much …"

"Get your coat. We're going to The Creamery."

CHAPTER 16

She could get used to life in apple country if all her evenings were like this. After their impromptu splurge at The Creamery, she and Greg walked along the dry Orchard Grove riverbed and then came home for a few rounds of chess. Katrina hadn't played before she met Greg, but she was already able to beat him one game out of every four or five. Not too bad.

"Want to watch a movie before bed?" Greg asked. They had both come home from their walk chilled and had changed their clothes. Katrina was in her pajamas. He was in flannel pants and a sweatshirt, and it wasn't even eight yet.

She couldn't remember when they last watched TV together. Sometime before the pregnancy probably. She wasn't even sure what kind of movies he liked. How could they be married but know so little about each other?

Her cell phone erupted into Tchaikovsky's *1812 Overture*. She and half the violin section in Long Beach had spent one evening at IHOP after rehearsal picking out various orchestral ringtones. She glanced at the phone and grimaced. *No. Anyone but that.*

Greg was staring at her. "Who is it?"

"Mrs. Porter. Probably something about the ..."

Greg grabbed her cell from her before she could react. "Hello, Pastor Greg speaking."

Katrina ignored the sinking disappointment in her stomach. Reminded herself what a good evening it had been. She studied Greg's features, trying to figure out from his expression if the conversation was going to turn hostile or not. For a moment, she imagined him explaining how she couldn't possibly be expected to direct a Christmas pageant, especially on such short notice. Maybe he'd step up and volunteer to do it himself. As if he didn't have enough obligations as it was.

"Yes, that's fabulous news." He cracked a smile and winked. A year ago, that simple gesture would have sent a flush zinging up to Katrina's cheeks. Now, she just felt tired.

"No, thank you. She'll be so excited to hear that." With as much as Greg was gushing, Katrina allowed her hopes to rise. Was the pageant cancelled? Had Mrs. Porter found somebody else to direct it? Somebody who could sing, who was comfortable with kids, and who didn't have an innate fear of public speaking? "That's so generous of you. Tell

Miles we appreciate his willingness."

Katrina thought through all the men at Orchard Grove Bible Church. Who in the world was Miles?

After making several more declarations of eternal gratitude and heaping praise upon Mrs. Porter's generosity, Greg hung up the phone, a smile still lighting up his face. "Good news, Mouse."

She tried to keep her expression serious. Reminded herself that with Mrs. Porter, you never knew if a gift was really a gift or some sort of poisonous barb. And Greg was such a people pleaser, she couldn't count on him to tell the difference.

"What is it?" she asked tentatively. Something wasn't right. If Mrs. Porter had cancelled the pageant, Greg would have responded differently, with plenty of *Are you sures?* and *It's really no problem for Katrina to take care of it.*

She'd allowed herself too much optimism. Now, as she watched her husband's crooked grin, she was sure of it.

"Guess." Was that honest excitement in his voice, or was he trying too hard? Was this all for some sort of show?

Whatever it was, Katrina was in no mood for twenty questions. "What?"

He patted the couch cushion, beckoning her to scoot closer to him. "So you know how it's been hard for you doing anything with the music since you're not a singer?"

She had no idea where this conversation was going, but she could already tell she wouldn't like its final destination. "Yeah?"

Now she was convinced his smile was exaggerated. After agreeing so enthusiastically with whatever Mrs. Porter was offering, he was having second thoughts now. He cleared his throat. "Well, Mrs. Porter's nephew Miles is the junior high and high school music teacher."

"So?"

He ran his palms over the knees of his flannel pants. "So, Miles has a little extra time with Christmas break coming up, and he's agreed to offer you singing lessons. Totally free. You start tomorrow."

CHAPTER 17

Stupid. Stupid to go into hysterics over something so minor. This time, Katrina didn't even need her husband to tell her she was overreacting.

Locked in the bathroom, ignoring Greg's questions on the other side of the door, she let the hot water from the shower scald her skin. Who cared if it wasted the parsonage's precious energy? With as little money as they paid her husband to begin with, the church would have no right to complain if they doubled their utility spending.

"Mouse, I just want to talk to you."

I'm not your mouse. She kept the thought to herself, knowing that she couldn't make her voice carry over the roar of the water and pounding of her husband's fists anyway. That's what she hated most about herself, how soft-spoken she remained even when she was full of rage, angry enough to kill.

What right did the church have to go behind her back and make arrangements for her to take voice lessons with a complete stranger?

She could just imagine how the conversation went. *Hey, Miles, you know that new pastor who's come into town and his wife that everyone's talking about because she's so young and used to be part of his youth group? Well, we really need her to direct our Christmas musical, and it would be nice if she could lead singing on Sunday mornings as well, but see, she can't sing a note to save her life. So why don't you go ahead and treat her like a charity case and whip her voice into shape. We'd all really appreciate it.*

The problem was when she told Greg she didn't want the lessons, he made it out like she was the one being unreasonable.

"They really care about you, Mouse. They want to see you take your musical gift and develop it."

What was it with every single person in this blasted town thinking that anybody who played second violin in a middle-rate symphonic orchestra should by extension know how to sing, lead worship, and direct a Christmas pageant? And what right was it of theirs to schedule her first lesson without consulting her? Not even Greg had thought to ask for her opinion. The entire church, including her husband, was in on the conspiracy.

And what would happen when all these petty gossips realized that two weeks of voice lessons wouldn't come close to turning Katrina into a singer? What then?

I suppose it's good she still has that violin of hers.

It was brave of her to try.

Maybe it's time for her to have a baby so she has something else to occupy her time and energy.

"Come on, Mouse. Let me in. Please."

She couldn't go on ignoring her husband forever, much as she might want to. She slammed off the water and plodded to the door. Who cared if she made puddles all over the stupid bathroom floor? At least nobody would complain about it at the next church business meeting because they wouldn't know.

She wrapped her towel around herself and threw open the door. "What?"

Greg was frowning, but instead of finding the anger she expected in his gaze, he looked concerned. He reached out and stroked her cheek. "You been crying?"

She shrugged. Some questions didn't warrant a response.

"Let's talk about it."

She walked past him toward their bedroom. "It'd be nice to get dressed first."

"Why? I like you just like that." She didn't turn around. Did he really think that sort of comment was appropriate at a time like this?

He followed her into the bedroom. "I guess I should have

asked you about the voice lessons before I agreed to it, huh?"

She kept her eyes focused on her pajamas laid out on the bed. "Might have been nice."

"It sounded like a really neat idea on the phone."

"Mmm."

He took in a deep breath and tried again. "I've heard you sing before. I think you have a sweet voice."

He was correct, in a way. If there was anything positive that could be said about Katrina's singing, it was sweet. In a quiet-to-the-point-of-being-timid, demure, and wispy sort of way. A breathy, airy voice with no power behind it.

At all.

And a two-week crash course crammed in over Christmas break wouldn't change any of that.

Greg sat down on the corner of the bed. "I'm sorry I didn't ask you first. Do you want me to call Mrs. Porter and cancel?"

She shook her head and buttoned the top of her nightgown. "No. It's too late now." She was about to go on, but his relieved sigh cut her off.

"I'm glad. Because I think these lessons might be a really good step for you. Maybe give you some confidence."

She pulled on her warm, fuzzy socks, ignoring that last remark. Two weeks. That's all Christmas break was. Two weeks.

Two weeks meeting with some stranger, humiliating herself most likely to the point of tears, but at least once she proved to the congregation that she simply couldn't sing, they'd stop pestering her about it.

This time for good.

CHAPTER 18

Katrina didn't realize that even schools as small as Orchard Grove had buzzers to let you into the building and strict sign-in procedures for all the guests. Even though she arrived five minutes after the school day ended, she still had to sign in at the office, then ask for directions twice so her voice could carry over the screams and shouts of all the students running to meet up with their friends or catch their busses home.

The door to the music room was only a few inches open, so she wasn't sure if she was supposed to knock or just go in. She rapped her knuckles against the wood, but the movement was so timid even she couldn't hear a sound. She nudged the door open with her foot. "Hello?"

She thought a school the size of Orchard Grove would have a smaller music room. She'd also been expecting a teacher like the older version of Mr. Holland, not a young man about her husband's age.

"You must be Katerina." He added the extra syllable to

her name like her Russian grandmother had.

She glanced at the floor. "Nice to meet you."

He was sitting behind a music stand. If this were the string section, he'd be the first violist. "Come in." He pulled out the seat next to him. "I hear you're quite the accomplished musician already."

She managed a slight smile and sat near him. One stand over and she'd be in her old spot from the symphony.

"So you just moved here from LA?"

"Long Beach." She wished she had her violin to hold against her chest like a shield. That was one reason she hated singing so much. With no instrument to hide behind, you were left absolutely exposed.

Naked.

"And you played in the symphony there, right? Violin?"

She nodded, wondering what it would be like to move to a town where every single resident didn't know her life history. What was he going to ask next? How old she'd been when she and Greg met? How long they waited from the time she graduated high school until their first date?

Instead, he stretched his arm across the back of the empty chair between them. So comfortable. So relaxed. "I'm a brass man myself. Trombone at first, just because they're the ones that lead the marching band, but I moved on to French horn once I discovered Tchaikovsky."

She smiled at him, the first time she didn't feel nervous enough to vomit since she'd pulled up to the school. "I love French horns."

"They say the French horn and the violin are the two instruments that come closest to matching the human voice."

Katrina had heard that same thing before but didn't want to sound like a know-it-all. "Wow, that's interesting."

"So tell me why you're here. You want to learn how to sing so you can lead music at your church?"

She despised the way her face would flush at the slightest provocation. If she hated singing, she hated talking about herself to a stranger just as much. "Something like that. Mrs. Porter, I mean your aunt ..."

He interrupted with a chuckle. "She can be a little overbearing at times. Is she the one who roped you into this?"

Katrina stared at her lap. There was no reason to deny it. "In a way."

Another small laugh. "Well, I'm sorry for your sake, but selfishly, I've been looking forward to this ever since she called me. I've been in Orchard Grove five years now, and I can't tell you how nice it is to have a real musician to work with for a change."

Another blush.

"Maybe one afternoon you can bring your violin, and I'll pull out my French horn, and we'll have a jam session."

Katrina tried to think up a quick excuse. She didn't do improv. Didn't like jazz. Didn't even play her violin anymore.

Thankfully, he didn't ask for a commitment. "So." He stood up and planted himself behind the piano. "Grab that bottle of water, come over here, and let's warm up your voice. I'm dying to hear what we have to work with."

CHAPTER 19

"You realize you haven't said more than two words to me since you got home, don't you?" Greg set down his fork and eyed Katrina.

She'd stayed longer than she'd planned at the school and had come home in time to boil some water and heat up a jar of spaghetti sauce. Since Greg couldn't last a single meal without some sort of meat on his plate, she'd also microwaved two polish sausages for him.

She filled her mouth with a forkful of spaghetti so she wouldn't be expected to talk as much. "Not much to say."

"You were there for over an hour," he remarked. "What'd you do that whole time? Do you think the lessons are going to help? What's your teacher like?"

"He's fine. We did mostly warmups. I have a few exercises I'm supposed to practice at home." For all the meals that Greg spent staring at the wall or stuffing his face without any regard for conversation, he was sure chatty tonight.

"Yeah?" he asked with a mouth full of noodles. "What

kind of exercises?"

"Just singing warmups. I might go over and do them at the church with the piano."

Greg shrugged. "You're welcome to use it any time. Just make sure the lights get turned off when you're done."

She wouldn't forget.

"So you think the lessons are going to help you with the pageant?"

"We'll see."

He frowned. "You're not very talkative."

What was she supposed to say? It had taken all her emotional energy and fortitude just showing up at that stupid school this afternoon. And then singing in front of a perfect stranger. Miles hadn't been discouraging, but she could tell from his reaction to her first warmup that he'd underestimated just how bad she was. Her mom was right. She simply couldn't sing.

Instead of meeting twice a week like they had initially planned, Miles suggested she come back daily so they could make the most of Christmas break.

She wasn't offended. She knew her voice needed work. She also knew that singing had far more to do with genetics than with discipline. Sure, she could do his silly exercises, meet with him twice a day for the next two weeks for all she cared, and she might make some slight improvements if she were lucky.

But in the end, she'd just be the shy pastor's wife with an off-key voice. How many times had her mom told her? The only real music she could ever make, the only real music she would ever make, was on her violin.

Her Dmitry, who lay abandoned and neglected in his velvet-lined case. It wasn't right. She thought that once she and Greg moved to Orchard Grove, she'd have more time to play than she had in Long Beach. Even if she found her muse again, it would take her months to make up for all the lost practice time. Months to fire her fingers back into shape.

Greg was looking moody in his seat at the table. She shouldn't have been ignoring him and thinking so much about her voice lessons. The more she could keep them out of her mind, the happier she'd be.

"Is dinner all right?"

He looked up from his plate. "Huh? What?"

"Dinner," she repeated. "Does it taste ok?"

He smiled and gave her a thumbs up before replying with a full mouth, "It's great. This sauce is terrific."

It was a good thing she sprang for that extra eighty cents to buy something besides the generic brand. Oh, well. At least he wasn't interrogating her about her singing anymore.

"What was your day like?" she asked. "You've hardly told me anything."

"It went fine." He dumped some more Parmesan cheese onto his plate. He'd used up nearly half the canister in this one meal. "The elders are having a meeting tomorrow. Want to know why we haven't gotten more kids showing up for youth group."

She didn't respond. After a lifetime spent in church, she had no idea how much drama went on behind the scenes, how the elders who were supposed to be the spiritual servants of the congregation could gang up against a young pastor like her husband. That's something she'd have to remind herself of when the Missionary League women like Mrs. Porter got on her nerves. At least she didn't have to answer to an entire board that got together two or three times a month to tell her every single thing she was doing wrong with her life and ministry.

It could always be worse.

She studied her husband, the weary crease lines across his forehead that she'd never noticed in California. He looked a full five years older than he had in their wedding pictures, the ones Greg still hadn't hung because he'd never bothered to get permission to put up one nail in the parsonage.

One nail.

Well, everyone had to pick their battles. Just like she did. She wouldn't fight against her voice lessons. Initially, she planned to show up just to get Mrs. Porter and anyone else with a stake in her training to shut up, but after her first meeting with Miles, she decided she might as well take advantage of the free training. It's not like she could have gotten a deal like this in Long Beach. And Miles, for all the times he could have made her feel bad for her breathy, insecure voice, acted like she at least possessed a shred of potential.

Why else would he have offered more lessons? It wasn't like he was getting anything out of it.

Greg looked at the time. "You about ready?"

Katrina had been thinking about those vocal warmups and arpeggios that had been running through her head all afternoon. Was there a business meeting tonight she'd forgotten about? "Ready for what?"

"For rehearsal." He stood up, leaving his plate of leftover spaghetti on the table. "Christmas pageant practice starts in ten minutes."

CHAPTER 20

She couldn't do this. Singing in front of a stranger was a harrowing enough experience for one day. Now she was the sole adult in charge of a room full of sixteen children, most of whom were far more interested in turning the shepherd staffs into swords than in any sort of singing or acting.

It was the most ill-prepared Katrina had been for anything. Half the time, she could hardly raise her voice loud enough to be heard. She was an even more pathetic director than she expected. Things were so bad that she was actually relieved when Mrs. Porter huffed her way downstairs "just to see how things were shaping up."

"I hate to admit it," Katrina confided, "but I don't really know what I'm doing."

Mrs. Porter clapped her hands for attention. and within three minutes each child had been issued a role in the pageant and a costume. The shepherd staffs still turned into weapons every now and then, but the kids were far more respectful of Mrs. Porter, a retired teacher most of them had known (and probably feared) their entire lives.

By the time the kids started practicing *Silent Night*, Katrina wondered why she was here at all. Mrs. Porter would make a much more efficient director than she could ever dream of being. She was so relieved to have someone else guiding the kids and making the decisions about the songs, the set, and the acting roles that she didn't feel marginalized when Mrs. Porter took over the hour-long rehearsal. With five minutes left before the kids got picked up, Katrina made her way to the bathroom upstairs, doubting Mrs. Porter or anyone else would even notice she was missing.

Quiet as a church mouse. That's how Greg described her when she slipped over from the parsonage to visit him while he worked in his church office. She'd done that far more during the first month or two at Orchard Grove, back when she didn't have to put on winter boots and a heavy coat just to walk a few steps outside. Back when her husband seemed happy to see her in the middle of his workday.

The bathroom door swung open while Katrina was still hidden in one of the stalls, and it was easy to identify the two speakers by their voices.

"What are you doing here, Nancy?" Mrs. Porter asked. They must have finished rehearsal a few minutes early. Either that or Katrina had been stalling here longer than she realized.

"I'm picking up DJ to take him home," the treasurer answered.

"That's awfully nice of you."

"It's the least I could do with Joy still suffering from her morning sickness like that. I know she's excited about growing her family, but you'd think they might learn to wait a little bit. You know, she's still nursing Brielle at night. No wonder she's so exhausted. I've told her it's not natural. And how are you? Are you here to pick someone up?"

Katrina was about to exit the stall but froze when the conversation turned toward her.

"No," Mrs. Porter said. "I stopped by to see how Katrina was doing with all those kids. She's got such a quiet presence, you know. I thought she might need some help."

"Did she?"

Mrs. Porter chuckled. "You could say that."

Nancy sighed. "Well, don't be too hard on her. She's young."

"I know that."

Katrina's palms were sweaty. By not coming out of the stall when she had the chance, she'd have to sit here for another five or ten minutes after these two women left, and even then she still might end up exposing herself as an eavesdropper.

Nancy lowered her voice. "Did you also know she and

Pastor Greg had a miscarriage?"

The sound of Mrs. Porter sucking in her breath was the only thing louder than Katrina's pulse pounding in her ears. "I knew she was pregnant!"

"We all did, ever since she got up to use the bathroom twice at that women's retreat. But something happened. They lost the baby, unfortunately."

"What a shame." Mrs. Porter clucked her tongue. "How far along was she, do you know?"

"Not very. I don't think she could have been past the first trimester. That's when I had my miscarriage."

Mrs. Porter let out a noisy sigh. "Mine too."

"Well, I'm sorry for the poor thing." There was a hint of true sympathy in Nancy's voice. "Here she is, away from her family for the first time. I imagine she must miss the orchestra or whatever it was she had down there in LA. Must be lonesome for her out in the middle of nowhere when she's used to the hustle and bustle of city life."

Katrina clenched every muscle in her body, terrified that some unwanted cough or clicking of teeth or other automatic noise would give her away. She waited several minutes after both women had left. Without thanking Mrs. Porter for taking over the rehearsal or bothering to hunt down her husband or her coat, she hurried outside to the welcoming privacy of the parsonage. She took out her violin, realized that even if she found the drive to play, her fingers were far too cold, and ended up polishing her instrument instead.

By the time Greg got home, Dmitry's wood glistened, Katrina's pulse had returned to a somewhat normal rate, and she felt ready to face another night home with her husband, pretending that everything was fine.

CHAPTER 21

Why should she feel nervous? This was her fourth singing lesson with Miles, and since it was a Saturday and the school was closed for Christmas, she didn't even have to worry about anyone stopping by or overhearing her if she allowed her voice to carry too far.

Surprisingly, she'd gotten comfortable around Miles over the past few afternoons. She'd been practicing her warmup exercises regularly. She'd always known that singing was controlled by your breath, but she hadn't realized how difficult it would be to access her diaphragm muscle to get it to behave the way it was supposed to.

"That's what's going to get you past your breathy voice and give you real *oomph* when you sing," Miles had assured her. It sounded so easy in theory, and it looked simple enough when he demonstrated. Miles' voice could be called a lot of things, but sweet certainly wouldn't be the first word that would come to anybody's mind.

As silly as she'd felt, she'd been practicing. Her progress

was measured in baby steps, but it was progress nonetheless.

There was no reason for her palms to sweat the way they did or for her heart to flutter this fast. Even the sound of Miles' French horn running through scales didn't drown out the thumping of her pulse.

She walked into the music room, this time without knocking, and Miles set down his instrument. "I didn't even hear you come in."

"You don't have to stop. It sounded nice."

He rewarded her compliment with a grin, so frank it was easy for Katrina to answer back with a smile of her own, forgetting momentarily how uneasy she'd felt walking down these quiet halls.

He glanced at her case. "So you brought it. I was hoping you wouldn't forget."

She wasn't sure what was supposed to happen now, or how bringing her violin to a voice lesson would turn her into a better singer. "Should I set up now?" she asked.

Miles shook his head. "Not quite yet. Let's do our warmups like normal. Then I want to try something new. I don't know if it will work, but I think we might have good success."

She nodded and made her way to the piano with the sheet of warmup music she'd been practicing from.

"You won't need this today." Greg took the paper out of

her hand and flashed another smile.

"What do you want me to sing, then?" Could he sense how terrified she was? She'd just gotten used to the page of scales, the endless *ma-ma-ma-ma-me* and *ooh-oo-aah* warmups he'd given her earlier in the week. And now he was moving her on to something different?

He played a simple C-major run on the piano. "Just follow me."

The warmup was similar to what she'd practiced before. More consonant sounds than she was used to, but otherwise not that different. What made it harder was this time he sang each note with her, working her vocal cords higher and higher up the scale. His voice was so strong, so powerful, that she didn't even make it a full octave before dropping out.

"Why'd you stop?" His gaze was piercing and refused to let her go.

"I don't know. I ..."

"You were doing great," he interrupted. "Why'd you quit?"

She licked her dry lips. "You were singing really loud. I didn't think I could keep up."

He shook his head. Replayed the last chord. "You went higher than this during our very first practice together. I know you have it in you."

She gave one more valiant effort but only managed to

progress two half-steps up the scale before she backed out again.

He rested his hands on the keyboard and stared at her. There was no judgement in his eyes, not even surprise. "What's going on?"

If he knew the answer, Katrina certainly didn't. "I'm not sure. It's ..." How could she explain it? Singing the warmup with him, even though it was only slightly more complicated than the ones she'd gotten used to earlier in the week ... It was like a first-year Suzuki student trying to play Tchaikovsky's violin concerto beside Itzhak Perlman. But she wasn't exactly sure how to express herself other than by saying, "I felt like your voice was drowning me out."

He smiled. She wondered if she would ever be as comfortable with others as he appeared to be with her. "I thought that was our problem."

She was ready for a pep talk, a lecture, another demand for her to try harder. What she didn't expect was for Miles to say, "Now get your violin out. I want to show you something."

Her hands were trembling. Miles knew she'd played for the Long Beach Symphony. What he didn't know was that she'd hardly picked up her instrument in months, and the times she did try to play usually ended in tears. She wished she had the confidence to explain to him, but instead she did as she was told, praying she wouldn't turn into a puddle of hysterics. This was her violin, her Dmitry. Her soulmate for years. After every fight with her mom, she'd poured her insecurities into her music, bowing out her sorrows. When she first developed a crush on her youth pastor, Dmitry had been her confidant. When impatience and longing burned hot in her core, her music had been her soul's only release. Her violin had soothed over every sorrow of hers except for one.

But she couldn't explain that to Miles. He was so good to take time out of his Christmas break to work with her, so kind to believe that she at least had some shred of potential or he wouldn't keep showing up. Whatever the musical hang-up was that had plagued her since the miscarriage, she'd have to put it aside for now. She was an adult, not a shy little girl.

She tuned up quickly, embarrassed that another musician might see how badly she'd neglected her instrument.

"You ready?" he asked.

No, she wasn't, but it was better to get it over with than stand here about to faint from nerves and dizziness.

"Your hands are shaking. Are you cold? They set the thermostat so low on the weekends."

She licked her lips. "I'm all right. Really." She wiped her hand on her pants, hoping he wouldn't notice how sweaty she'd already made her fingerboard. "So what do you want me to do?"

"You're going to do that warmup we just did, but I want you to play it on your violin. Think you can do that by ear, or do you need me to write out the notes?"

She wasn't sure if he was joking, so she didn't laugh. "I don't need the notes. Thanks."

"Ok." He started back down at middle C, playing the run once through as if she didn't already have it seared into her mind. "I'm going to be singing with you, got it? And this time, you better be the one to drown me out."

She gave him a quick nod. Not the kind you give to answer a yes or no question. The kind of nod you offer to your stand partner when it's time for a page turn. Or the gesture you make when you're playing with a string quartet and you and the cellist need to come in at just the same moment.

That quick tilt of the chin that feels so natural when you have a violin planted firmly on your shoulder. An extension of your arm. And, if you play openly enough, an extension of your very soul.

He sang with her while her fingers ran up the strings. He was wrong. She wasn't supposed to drown him out. Where would be the musicality in that? Instead, she let her violin adjust to his pitch, his expression, his voice.

His tone changed. Not that it gained volume so much as intensity. If she'd been trying to sing with him, nobody would be able to hear her even if she had a microphone. But now, with her violin matched to his voice, their instruments in sync, the power of his voice didn't drown her out but summoned even more passion, more focus, more energy to her music.

Her hands were sweaty still, but this time from the exertion. There wasn't a hint of nervousness, not a trace of the shyness that had always permeated the space between her and her teacher. Nothing but the music.

Fervent. Impassioned.

Raw.

She was on the E string now, working her way higher up the fingerboard. This time, it was he who stopped first. "Sorry. I'm no tenor."

She was breathless but hoped he didn't notice. It wasn't supposed to happen like this. There was a closeness that came when two people poured themselves into their music. An unspoken bond. That was why listening to a string quartet felt so much more intimate, almost voyeuristic. What made the Long Beach Symphony feel like a family?

She lowered her violin from her shoulder, wondering what was supposed to happen next. The air zinged with the music they had just created. The moment they had just shared.

Ethereal.

She didn't look away when his gaze landed on her. Funny how you could learn so much about a person through the music they made, how you could sense the passions, the longings, the past sorrows. None of it could be put into words, of course. It could only be felt, an intangible sense you can't describe or explain away.

He reached for her instrument. Not even her own husband had handled her violin before, but Miles was a musician. She could trust him. She let go of Dmitry, surrendering her beloved instrument and her bow.

"Now," he said, "sing it again. Without me this time. I'll give you the starting note. You do the rest."

And she did. It was nothing like the magic they had just created, but it was measurable progress from her feeble attempts earlier. When she finished, the room echoed brightly with the ringing sound.

"Hear that?" he asked.

She nodded, wishing to be hidden once more behind her violin. Wishing to be shielded from her teacher's frank stare. Her lungs were full, but she wasn't tired or drained, just energized. Excited.

She glutted herself on oxygen, taking a breath from deep in her gut. Whatever tricks Miles had been trying to teach her about using her diaphragm properly had been lost on her until now.

Until this moment.

She was still no diva. She had the self-awareness to recognize that. She'd never sing a solo on Broadway or audition for the stage.

But something had happened. As much as singing was about breathing, she realized it was also about confidence. Security. She could have never let a noise like that pass through her own throat if she hadn't felt completely safe. Maybe she was getting used to Miles and his teaching style. Maybe she felt freer knowing that there were no students here over the weekend.

Maybe playing her violin had awakened her musical passion again.

The reason itself was insignificant. What mattered was that she'd done it. Created the elusive moment where your music is so open, so real, so raw that there's nothing between you and your listener. No filter, no self-censoring between your soul and his.

Not only that, but she'd proven her mom wrong. She'd spent her entire life too terrified to sing in front of anybody, but now everything had changed.

Katrina had found her voice.

CHAPTER 22

"You're awfully chipper tonight," Greg remarked as Katrina sneaked her way onto his lap during dinner.

"I just wanted to reach the butter."

His fingers lingered on her neck and traveled down her back. "I could have passed it to you."

She kissed him on the cheek. "Where would be the fun in that?"

"What's gotten into you?" he asked as she squirmed off him and back into her own seat.

"Nothing. I just wanted the butter." There was no use trying to hide her smile.

He looked so handsome. That dimple on the bottom of his chin, those broad shoulders. She'd known him for so long, and never did he look more irresistible than right now.

"Why do you keep staring at me like that?" he asked, even though the playful twinkle in his eyes told Katrina he knew exactly what she was doing, and he liked it.

"No particular reason," she teased.

"You keep looking at me that way, you're going to end up with more than just butter."

She smiled coyly. "Maybe that's what I'm hoping for."

He reached across the table for her when his phone rang. Stupid cell. For a second, she was naïve enough to think he might let it go to voicemail.

"Hello, this is Pastor Greg."

No such luck.

She sighed and sank back in her chair, gnawing on the three day-old bread roll that tasted remarkably bland considering how much attention she'd given to smothering it with butter.

"No," Greg was saying, "you weren't interrupting anything … Yeah, we're eating dinner, but we're nearly finished up. The meal's practically over. What did you need?"

He got up without even sparing Katrina a glance and retreated to his office, leaving her alone with a table full of cold food, dirty dishes, and a stale piece of bread.

CHAPTER 23

From the sound of Greg's muffled voice on the other side of his office door, Katrina guessed whoever called wasn't very happy. Greg was using his placating tone, the one he'd perfected whenever he was apologizing to someone at the church for failing to shovel the walkway or making excuses for his wife who'd allegedly left a light on in the church basement.

Any thoughts she'd held about making tonight sweet and romantic were lost. Oh, well. Something had happened in her today, a spark or awakening that she couldn't explain. When she'd gotten home from her voice lessons, she'd jumped straight into cooking dinner, but now that she had a little extra time, she wanted to play her violin. Alone this time. See if somehow Miles' magic that had unlocked her diaphragm, giving her the confidence to sing like she never imagined she could, had also freed her from whatever mental or creative block was keeping her from making music with Dmitry like she used to.

She wasn't even sure which she was more excited for,

practicing her new vocal runs or pulling out her violin. She scribbled a quick note for her husband and headed over to the church, clutching her case against her chest as if it were a baby she was trying to protect from the cold.

Snow fell lightly around her. Once Greg got off the phone with whoever he was apologizing to, he'd be out here salting and shoveling so it'd be ready for church tomorrow. The whole night stretched out before her. A night with just her, Dmitry, and if she felt like it, her voice.

All evening, thoughts of her lesson with Miles snaked through her mind. Sometimes subtle, like in the first bars of Peer Gynt tiptoeing *In the Hall of the Mountain King*, sometimes racing like in the piece's climax. The amazing part was realizing that her potential, the sound she'd made as it rang through the music room, had been with her throughout her entire life. All her mom's berating about her voice had been a lie. All Katrina needed was a guide to help her access the gift she had been given.

Miles hadn't handed her a magic potion that transformed her little mousy voice into an instrument of power and ringing clarity. All he'd done was lead her to the part of her spirit where she could tap into that ability herself.

Now the biggest question remaining was whether or not she could replicate that performance when she was by herself.

She let herself into the church, careful to shut and lock the door behind her.

There was a piano up on the stage in the sanctuary, but she wasn't ready for that yet. She needed a more enclosed space. To recreate the way she'd sung earlier today, she needed to feel safe. She needed to feel protected.

There was a small keyboard in the cry room, which was hardly more than a closet attached to the back of the sanctuary for mothers to sit with their fussy babies. It would do for a start, at least until she got her voice warmed up.

She played a C chord, then hummed the first few runs Miles had taught her. She was afraid that what happened today was a once-in-a-lifetime event or something that could only be recreated when Miles was nearby. But after a few minutes, when she got used to the sound of her own tentative singing, she allowed herself to reach into that breath she'd so recently discovered, that place in her gut where her diaphragm apparently connected to her psyche and propelled out the music of her soul.

It wasn't quite as ringing as it had been at the school, but that could be explained by the open, gym-like acoustics of Miles' music room. Even though the sound here wasn't exactly as clear, she felt the passion just the same. The boldness. She hadn't realized until now that she'd been living life afraid of her own voice. After hearing what she could do, she didn't want to cover it up again.

She wasn't ready to jump in front of the church and sing a solo, but maybe with practice she'd even overcome that fear. It could start small. Singing with the kids during the Christmas pageant. Allowing her voice to carry more than two inches in front of her during Sunday morning worship, even on those days when she wasn't on stage and had nothing to do with the singing.

It was hard to overestimate what Miles had done for her. Once her husband got off his phone call and finished shoveling, if he wasn't in a horrid mood already, she wanted to find a way to explain it. Maybe one day she'd feel comfortable singing for him. It was a start, a step toward sharing this new gift she'd discovered with others.

Twenty minutes later, she needed to stop. She hadn't brought over any water or tea, wasn't particularly hydrated to start with, and as exciting as it was to have this newfound power within her, the truth was that her voice was still new and inexperienced. She had to take a break.

The cry room was perfect for a timid singer who wanted to feel enclosed, but it was far too small for a violinist, especially one who swayed as much as she did. That wasn't a problem, though, since she'd been playing her violin on stages and in wide open concert halls for almost her entire life. She walked into the sanctuary, checking twice to make sure she'd turned off the lights in the cry room, and inhaled deeply. She didn't know what it was about Miles' method of breathing instruction, but she'd never felt so healthy or strong. She'd recently read a study saying that singing just ten minutes a day could extend your life. She'd attributed that to the healing power of music itself, but maybe it had just as much to do with the breathing as anything else.

Whatever it was, this was a feeling she didn't want to lose. Like a newlywed couple never going back to just kissing. There was only forward from here. She didn't want to be silenced again.

She took out her bow first, confident as she rosined him up. This was an upgrade, a bow that was even more expensive than the violin she'd owned before Dmitry. They'd only been together for a little over two years, but he and Dmitry acted like soulmates separated for half a lifetime and only now finding each other again.

And now Dmitry was under her chin. He'd stayed relatively in tune since his trip to the school this afternoon. Just a few minor adjustments on the higher strings. And then she was ready to play.

If she'd been nervous about resuming her relationship

with her violin after such a long hiatus, she'd been worrying over nothing. Like a couple pulled away from each other for a few short, painful months and then tossed back into their bed of passion and intimacy, she was one with her instrument. He wasn't even an extension of her. He was her. Slow, rusty fingers, cramped wrists, awkward bowings — there had been nothing to worry about at all. Why had she neglected him for so long? Why had she ignored the one friend who could truly understand her sorrows and turn each tear into music, a prayer without words that expressed the hidden depths of her soul?

She'd been afraid of so many things. Of playing her violin again after losing her child. Of flashbacks of the trip to the emergency room. Scared even of her grief.

She was tired of being afraid. She was tired of being a little church mouse who squeaked in terror at every sound. Why should she be so fearful? Sure, she was young, but she was an adult. An accomplished musician who knew more about city life and sophistication than just about anyone else in Orchard Grove.

There was no reason to be afraid.

Even her music reflected this new confidence. New boldness. Katrina's playing had always been lyrical, both mournful and beautiful. *Soul-aching*, one of the Solo and

Ensemble judges had told her back in high school. A few other violinists in her district had achieved more technical skill, but none of them could make their instruments sing like Katrina could. None of them could reach out and connect with their audience in a way that was so open and raw. Another judge called her music *haunting*.

But now, the lyrical, drawn-out beauty of her instrument was replaced with something new. Boldness and confidence. Fast, almost flirtatious. Her fingers sprinted up and down the board like her voice had so recently run through her practice riffs. Katrina had always preferred playing in the lower registers, where she could make Dmitry sing mournfully. When she had to play up high, she did so almost apologetically.

Squeaking, like she once had with her voice.

No more. Whatever had been unlocked in her singing today had transferred to her violin. She wasn't just playing Dmitry after taking a few months off and picking up right where she had left off. She was a new musician.

No, that wasn't the right way to put it. She could still do the lyrical and haunting tones, but there was another layer — another whole world — that opened up to her now. She'd always hated Mozart, thought his violin parts were ridiculously pompous and bombastic, but now as she played through the opening of his third violin concerto,

ALANA TERRY

she realized how strong she felt.

This is what it meant to play without any fear or any inhibitions at all. *If only my friends at the symphony could hear me now.* Katrina was deaf to the sanctuary acoustics which had so often irked her in the past. She was ignorant of the fact that she was playing so loud anybody walking down the sidewalk could hear her clearly.

There was no more sanctuary. There was no more Orchard Grove.

For the first time since she and Greg packed up his car and moved to this barren town, she wasn't bound by the traditionalism, the judgmental attitudes or catty gossip. She wasn't held down by fears or anxieties or worries about what others would think of her.

None of that could hold her down anymore.

Katrina was free.

CHAPTER 24

It wasn't until she heard the pounding on the door and glanced at the clock that she realized she'd been playing for over two hours. Unlike her voice, which could only withstand fifteen or twenty minutes of hard and focused practice, on her violin she felt like she was only warming up.

She hurried to the church entrance, wondering who would be stopping by. It was after eight, which in Orchard Grove time was akin to about eleven in the city. The sun had set, and glancing out the window she noticed that Greg had already shoveled the walkway.

Why hadn't he called her home sooner? Was he mad she'd come over here?

She opened the door with an apology on her tongue, except it wasn't Greg.

"Miles?"

He smiled down at her. How was it that she hadn't realized how tall he was until now?

"I was jamming with some buddies at the school this

evening, and I realized you'd left your coat." He held it out to her. She'd been so focused on his height and her surprise seeing him there that she hadn't even noticed it in his hands.

"I figured I'd take it to your house," he explained, "but then I parked and heard the music in here. It was breathtaking. Are you a fan of Mozart?"

"Not until recently," she admitted and realized that standing here with the door open was exposing her wooden violin to the extreme temperature as well as leaking heat out of the sanctuary. "Sorry, I don't want to get him too cold. Want to step in for a minute?"

"Him?" Miles asked with a smile.

Katrina wasn't sure what he was referring to.

"You called your violin a him," he explained.

"Oh, yeah." A flush warmed her cheeks.

"It's all right. My French horn's a beautiful, foxy lady named Nadine."

Katrina tried to hide her giggle.

"Go ahead and laugh."

"No, it's not you. It's just that my husband thinks it's strange I've named my instrument." She looked back to find him staring at her. What was it about his gaze that made her feel so vulnerable and safe at the same time? "It's nice to know I'm not the only one," she finished lamely and turned back around.

She was at the front of the church now. Her plan was to put Dmitry down, take her coat, and say goodnight, but Miles draped her coat over one of the pew backs and showed no interest in leaving.

"You come over to practice a lot?"

"Not really. I mean sometimes." She set her violin down only to pick him back up again a few seconds later. "I haven't played much in a few months."

"Winter blues?"

"Hmm, what? Oh, no. Nothing like that. At least I don't think so." Why was she stammering all of a sudden? He shouldn't be here. Even if Greg was too busy right now to notice it was dark and late and past time for her to have returned home, each minute she lingered put her at risk of being discovered here alone with another man.

So much for that newfound sense of boldness.

She pulled out her silk rag and started wiping her fingerboard clean.

"Don't wrap things up on my account." Miles was right next to her now. Looking down at the bow that trembled slightly in her hands. "I didn't mean to cut your practice time short."

"No, it's just that I'd lost track of time. I really should

head home. My husband might start to wonder where I've gone." She let out an unconvincing laugh and hurried to set Dmitry into his case.

"Wait." Miles' hand was on hers now. Keeping her from strapping her violin in place. "You sounded so good from outside. Won't you play for me just once?"

She glanced at the clock again. His hand was still gripping hers. She stood staring with her mouth open like some sort of idiot as Miles leaned toward her.

As if he hadn't been close enough already.

"One piece?" His breath was hot on her ear. He reached an arm across her. Was he trying pull her in, or was he just keeping her coat from falling off the back of the pew?

Katrina took in a deep breath, the kind that was powered completely by her diaphragm just like he'd taught her. She wasn't some little church mouse without a voice. Chances were that he had no idea how uncomfortable he was making her, and until she found a way to tell him, she'd be nothing more than the shy, speechless creature she'd been when they first met.

Her body trembled once, and he was pressed in so near she was certain he must have felt it. She pulled her hand away from his and took a step away. "I need to go home," she declared, infusing her words with strength, conviction, and that all-important breath. "My husband is waiting for me."

CHAPTER 25

If Greg had been worried about Katrina spending hours tonight at the church, he refused to show it. She'd been in the dining room for ten minutes before he emerged from his office.

"What are you doing, Mouse? I thought you were practicing."

She kept her back to him and glanced over her shoulder. "Just cleaning up after dinner."

"Everything ok?" There was a hint of concern in his voice that might have been endearing if he'd come out and asked that question as soon as she walked in the door.

After Miles left, she decided to tell her husband everything. About the music, about his strange visit. But during the minute and a half it took to walk from the pulpit to the back door to the parsonage, she'd lost all her resolve. First of all, there was nothing about the musical encounter she'd experienced today with Miles that her guitar-player of a husband would come close to understanding. Second of all, if she made a big deal about her teacher's behavior in the sanctuary, there's no way Greg would listen to the story and leave it at that.

There'd be questions, anger, jealousy. And what for? What was so weird about a man stopping by to drop off a coat his student had forgotten at their lesson? A lesson in which they'd made music together with a harmony, an energy that even the most untrained listener could detect?

The whole thing was a big misunderstanding. Miles asked her to play a simple song, she mistook his request, somehow twisted it into the realms of impropriety, and why? A year ago, during her days with the Long Beach Symphony, there would have been nothing questionable about two musicians staying after practice, making a little music together, showing off what they'd been working on. Why had she made such a big deal over nothing?

She'd been rude too. Miles hadn't argued with her, hadn't acted mad, but she could tell he was surprised. All he'd wanted was one song. Why did she have to go and turn it into something shameful?

And why did her ear still burn where his breath had fallen on her?

Katrina carried the plate of stale buns into the kitchen only to realize her husband was still waiting for a reply.

"I'm fine." She couldn't remember the exact question

but figured this was a pretty safe response. Summoning up her new sense of boldness, she met her husband's gaze. "What's wrong? Was I out too late?"

He shook his head. "No, you've just been acting strange all evening. You haven't played your violin at the church in months, and earlier you ..."

"I would have played here, but I thought you were on a work call. I didn't want to make too much noise."

"That's not the problem."

"Then what is?" She hadn't meant to sound so testy, but now she realized that it was her husband's fault things got so awkward with Miles. If she hadn't been so worried about him walking over, misconstruing what she was doing there with a man in the sanctuary, she wouldn't have been so rude. She could have played a piece for her teacher, they could have talked for a few more minutes, and that would be the end of it.

Greg shook his head. "Never mind. I'm probably just overreacting."

She crossed her arms. *You think?* She knew better than to say the words out loud.

He pulled out a chair and sat down at the table while Katrina continued to clean up their mess from dinner. "I'm sorry, Mouse. It's just that the elders are breathing down my neck again. I'm probably not in the best of moods right now. I wasn't trying to pick a fight or anything."

Katrina tried to remember. Had her husband ever apologized this readily to her at any point in the past?

"That's ok," she told him, thankful that her clearing job gave her something to do so she wouldn't have to meet his eyes. "What's going on with the elders, anyway?" What she should have said was *what is it this time?* but she wasn't sure how helpful that sort of phrasing would be.

"It's that stupid pageant. Mrs. Porter's ticked because she felt shanghaied into helping when you ..."

"I didn't ask that woman to lift a pinky last night." Katrina slammed the bowl full of leftover peas on the counter. "I didn't invite her. I didn't ask her to butt in."

Greg shook his head. "No, but apparently you left halfway into the rehearsal and didn't even stick around to see if all the kids got picked up."

Katrina opened her mouth to argue back, but he was basically right.

He sighed. "I know Mrs. Porter's a difficult person to deal with. She's got her own idea of how to run things. What do you expect? She was a teacher and then a principal for decades. She's used to bossing people around and getting her own way."

It wasn't fair. First the woman intruded on the rehearsal, assumed the role of director since apparently Katrina wasn't doing a good enough job, and then she had the audacity to complain when Katrina left five minutes early?

"Listen." Greg's voice was soft, more defeated than argumentative, but for once in their marriage Katrina was itching for a good fight. A yelling match. Any outlet where she could focus all this irritation and rage. "We've talked about this before. Appearances mean a lot here. We really need to make it a point to be the first people in and the last ones to leave whenever they've got something going on. Ok? I know Mrs. Porter's a pain, but that's part of our job description. It's just something we need to put up with."

She had plenty to say in response. Remind him that it was his name on the contract, his name on the checks, his name on the paystubs, not hers. This wasn't her job. The church didn't hire her. They didn't pay into her Social Security account or force her to keep office hours or write her a job description.

That's because the job description for the role of pastor's wife at a church like Orchard Grove would cost too much ink and take up too much paper than the stingy elders here were willing to dish out. A job description that didn't just require her to call in the nursery workers, fill in at a moment's notice anytime someone failed to show, lead music with her husband whenever the pianist was out of town, attend every single stupid women's luncheon and fundraising tea the Missionary League organized, and direct the children's Christmas pageant. Her job description also required her to be the first one in and the last one out every time the church opened, the one to make sure all the lights got turned off properly, the only woman who was expected to wear both a dress and nylons every single Sunday of the year, to be on call to play her violin at will as if she were some sort of street-corner musician taking requests.

And all this without pay and simply because she'd fallen in love with the man the folks at Orchard Grove wanted to call their pastor.

What plumber's wife was expected to arrive with him to every job looking pretty and clean and ready to work at a moment's notice? What teacher's spouse was expected to be the first one into the classroom and the last one out each day as well as the one to lock everything up properly when all was said and done? Was a doctor's wife expected to clean up the exam tables or babysit the kids in the waiting room or take the temperature for all her husband's patients?

There were so many thoughts, so many arguments, so many complaints running through Katrina's head, but she knew if she started to tell her husband everything that was on her mind, she would lose any sense of self-control. And how could she expect him to take her seriously then? Cursed hormones. Cursed town.

She hated being a pastor's wife. Hated it with an intensity she hardly recognized in herself. Hated the pressure to look perfect, act perfect, be perfect. And no matter what she did, even if she was doing everything right, someone would still complain that it wasn't good enough.

There would always be someone pointing out all her mistakes, talking behind her back about all her shortcomings. Just like in the bathroom at the pageant rehearsal. She could tell Greg about what happened. At least explain why she left church early. But there was no way she could make it through the story without tears. The humiliation was so deep, the wounds still fresh. And she hated crying in front of him. Hated it because he always tried to comfort her. He didn't realize that her tears were almost always now tears of anger, but he'd jump in and do what he could to cheer her up. Kiss her boo-boo and make it all better.

She should have never agreed to come here. She should have never thought she could make it as a pastor's wife, not at a church like this.

Her mom had tried to warn her, hadn't she? But Katrina never listened.

If she'd known what kind of town they'd end up in, if she'd had any sort of inkling of what type of reception was waiting for her at Orchard Grove Bible Church, could all the love in the world have convinced her to follow Greg here?

Or should she have taken her mom's advice and just stayed home? The thought was dark, oppressive, and ugly, but the more she examined it, the more she wondered if it was true.

Maybe she would have ended up happier if she hadn't married him at all.

CHAPTER 26

Nobody had made her feel this way before. Loved. Cherished. Desired.

Heat burned in the core of her body. Passion fanning passion into flame.

Even though she had every reason to suspect this was a dream, she didn't want to wake up.

He was everything she wanted. Everything she needed.

She'd never felt so safe. Protected.

Even in her sleep, she didn't want to open her eyes. Didn't want to somehow bring an end to this perfection.

But she did. And the man staring down at her was not her husband.

CHAPTER 27

It was nothing to feel guilty about. She was glad that it was Sunday, glad that Greg was already awake and most likely over at the church office by the time her brain snapped her out of whatever fantasy she'd dived into in her sleep.

It's not like she had conscious power over her thoughts while she slept. How can you be accountable for something you can't even control?

If Greg were here, he'd know. She could never face him when she felt guilty. That's why she'd been so quick to go to bed last night, even to the point of swallowing down her pride and apologizing for leaving rehearsal early just so they could get to the part where they stopped talking about it.

Stopped thinking about it.

Which is exactly what Katrina needed to do right now. Sunday school would start in a little over an hour. After the embarrassing disaster last week, she'd made a commitment to make the house at least somewhat presentable every Sunday morning just in case her husband invited someone over. But with as bad of a mood as he'd been in last night after that phone call with the elders, maybe he wouldn't be feeling particularly sociable today.

It was worth hoping for.

Was it bad for her to secretly rejoice when Greg got stressed at work? Maybe then he'd finally realize what a lousy job this was. They should have known from the start. How many pastors had come to serve at Orchard Grove in the past decade? From what she could recall, none of them had made it a full calendar year.

Now that she'd been here, it was obvious why.

She jumped in the shower, ready to wake up her brain, which was still longing to crawl back to bed even though that's the last thing she needed right now. She'd read about some women having dreams like that but had never experienced one herself.

She had to get it out of her mind. Mental bleach. Why couldn't that be a real thing? If she had time, she'd play her violin. But what if that only reminded her of him?

So no violin. There had to be a new plan. Shower, clean, and pray. Pray hard. Pray for God to forgive her for whatever sinful thoughts had crept into her head, with or without her permission last night. Pray that her husband would never find out about her mental meanderings, pray that the man from her dream would get called mysteriously off to someplace far away and preferably in a different time zone, and most importantly, pray that God would erase the memory of that dream, that touch, that perfect bliss, from her mind completely.

Was that so much to ask?

CHAPTER 28

She was late for Sunday school. Even after all Greg's lecturing last night about how she was always supposed to be the first one to church and the last one out, even when the walk from her front door to the downstairs Sunday school room was less than a hundred steps away, she ended up coming in and slipping into her chair right after her husband finished his opening prayer.

He glanced at her, but she couldn't tell if his expression was one of concern or anger. She wouldn't worry about that. Whatever he felt about her tardiness, she couldn't do anything to change it now. Realizing she'd forgotten her Bible at home, she reached out timidly for one of the extras stacked on the table in front of her, keenly aware of two dozen sets of eyes staring at her.

What kind of pastor's wife shows up late to Sunday school?

What kind of pastor's wife leaves her Bible at home?

What kind of pastor's wife has a very intense, very realistic, and horrifically inappropriate dream about her voice teacher?

She did her best to blink away the headache creeping up behind her eyes. She'd never gotten headaches in Long Beach, not one, but now they were an every-week occurrence, sort of like her fights with Greg about the utility bill at the parsonage. She glanced at her husband, who was now lecturing about the historical background of the church of Galatia. She'd been so young when she first fell for him.

Talk about inappropriate.

But she'd waited. They'd waited. Even though her attraction started years earlier, Greg told her several times it hadn't been until she was halfway through her senior year that he first noticed her as anything other than another girl in his youth group.

And even then it was two more years before they started dating. The months leading up to their wedding felt like such a blissful blur. Falling in love. Realizing that the man she'd been infatuated with for half of her teen years no longer saw her as a child and was in love with her too. Tearful nights crying into his shoulder because her mom was being so unreasonable about their relationship. Hurrying off to get married almost as soon as they got engaged so her mom couldn't do anything more to stop them.

Sometimes she still couldn't believe it. She was married to this man. This man she'd loved for years.

Only the marriage was nothing like she'd planned. When Greg mentioned moving back to the town where he'd grown up, Orchard Grove had felt so exciting. So exotic.

So far away from her caustic mother who would try to poison their marriage for as long as they remained within driving distance.

Somewhere to start a new life, a new beginning with her husband.

They should have never left Long Beach. At least there she'd be busy with rehearsals during the weeknights. Something to get her out of the house, a way to connect with her friends in the orchestra.

Her family.

Greg was discussing Paul's greeting in the first chapter of the book of Galatians, but his voice had become so grating over the past few months Katrina did her best to tune him out. Think about happier times. Purer times.

When she and Greg were just starting to date, just beginning to fall in love, imagining a future that seemed so promising, so beautiful, and so far off in the distance. Like a dream.

Except now, the dream had ended, reality had set in, and all Katrina wanted to do was find a way to put herself back to sleep.

CHAPTER 29

"Katrina, sweetheart." Something about the words stopped her cold.

She turned around. Mrs. Porter was frowning at her with a look that was all sympathy. "I just heard what happened." She wrapped her arms around her neck and planted a noisy, sloppy kiss on her cheek. "I'm so sorry, sweetie. That's terrible. You must be devastated."

Katrina was so surprised she could do nothing but blink when Mrs. Porter released her hold.

"You need to let your body rest and recuperate."

The miscarriage. It had taken Katrina's brain that long to figure out what Mrs. Porter was babbling on about so profusely. That's right. Nancy Higgins had leaked the news in the bathroom on Wednesday. It had probably made its way to the prayer chain by now. Katrina had been so focused on her music over the past few days she hadn't thought quite so much about the miscarriage. It's possible that if it weren't for all these old gossips, she might have been able to move on entirely instead of having her wounds ripped clean off the very second they started to heal over.

Mrs. Porter was talking so loudly that several other women came over and reached out to stroke Katrina's hair, shoulders, and back. Stupid of her to think a secret like hers could have ever stayed hidden in Orchard Grove.

"Of course, I'll take over the pageant." Mrs. Porter's words were met with emphatic nods and enthusiastic murmurs of approval. "There's no reason for you to worry your pretty little head about that. You just rest up and let your body heal."

A woman with coffee on her breath stepped forward. "Miscarriages can be terrible things, but God always knows what's best, doesn't he?"

A whole new round of unanimous assent, even more boisterous than before.

"It probably means there was something wrong with the child."

"At least now you know you can get pregnant. Hopefully next time it will be a healthy one."

"Good thing it happened early before you had the chance to get attached."

"Don't worry. You and PG are young enough you can always try for another."

Try for another. As if the dead child she'd been mourning was nothing but a dress rehearsal.

"Come on now." Nancy Higgins' voice carried over the sympathetic droning. "Give the poor thing some room to breathe." She pushed her way into the circle of perfume and floral patterns and permed hair and wrapped an arm protectively around Katrina's waist. "Don't let them get to you," she whispered into Katrina's ear and then addressed the small crowd. "It's time to head upstairs. You know PG likes to start right on time."

The gaggle of women who had previously been so smotheringly concerned about Katrina's reproductive history now dispersed without sparing her another glance. Three of them talked about the sale on wooden frames at the craft store as they headed upstairs, and a couple others discussed whether the Christmas tree should be taken down before or after New Year's.

Katrina blinked at Nancy, the only other woman who remained downstairs.

"You looked shell-shocked there," Nancy remarked. "Thought I might give you a little help."

It would have been infinitely more helpful if Nancy had never told anyone about the miscarriage in the first place, but as much as Katrina wanted to say so, she couldn't find her voice.

"By the way, before we head up, I wanted to ask you something." Nancy paused with her hand on the banister. "Did you have a friend over last night? I was dropping off some winter coats for the women's shelter downstairs. Let myself in the back door, and I could have sworn I heard you talking to someone."

If there was ever a time for Katrina to overcome her propensity to blush, this was it. She straightened her spine. "Yes, I'm taking singing lessons with Miles Porter from the school."

Nancy offered a quizzical look, one Katrina couldn't decipher, and said, "Oh." She turned around and without another word went up the stairs.

Katrina followed, silent as usual.

As quiet as a little church mouse.

CHAPTER 30

There was a reason she hadn't wanted to let anyone here know about the miscarriage. Greg would never understand. He thought that the more you talked about your loss, the faster you could move on.

That's not the way Katrina's heart or brain were wired. She was introspective, like the Virgin Mary who didn't go off blabbing to every single shepherd or wise man or prophet but *treasured up all these things and stored them in her heart.*

Katrina was intensely private and had been for her entire life. It made sense after growing up with a mother whose working philosophy was never say anything that might shed suspicion on the family. Might make people doubt that everything was perfect behind the closed doors of their small Bellflower mansion.

If you suffered at all, if your mother was so overbearing that you fell victim to debilitating panic attacks nearly every day of your childhood, you didn't acknowledge it. Instead, you got yourself an inhaler and told people you were asthmatic.

If you fell in love with a dirt-poor youth pastor from Hicksville, Washington, you ignored your feelings, dumped him, and moved on with your life. At least that's what Katrina's mother expected her to do.

And if your daughter elopes with said dirt-poor youth pastor, you make every threat possible to try to force her to have an annulment until she and her new husband run off to another state just to get away from you. And you'll never breathe a word about the marriage to anyone in your social circle, going so far to protect your own reputation that on the occasional times you actually send her letters at her new home, you insist upon using her maiden name.

That's the kind of privacy Katrina grew up with. The kind of secretiveness that wouldn't dream of broadcasting news about something as personal as a miscarriage to the entire community. There probably wasn't a single soul in all of Orchard Grove now who hadn't heard about what happened to her.

Just when she'd started to move on ...

She felt guilty now that she hadn't thought about her baby as much in the past few days. She'd finally gotten over the block that was keeping her from playing her violin. Didn't that victory count for anything?

Not anymore. Not with the entire town of Orchard Grove

reminding her of what she'd lost, with all the Missionary League women offering unsolicited tidbits of comfort that were about as useful as pouring salt water on a two-inch deep gash.

At least now you know you can get pregnant? Had those words seriously come out of someone's mouth? It was almost as bad as *you can always try for another.*

She gritted her teeth as she made her way into the sanctuary. The decorations were so gaudy she couldn't wait to fast-forward through the Christmas season. Well, at least now she was relieved of her responsibilities for the pageant. That was one good thing that came out of all this.

Did Greg know? Did he have any idea of how his wife had been accosted just a few minutes earlier? Or was he too busy shaking hands and pretending to be the picture-perfect, happy preacher the folks at Orchard Grove thought they hired? She hated how fiercely loyal he was to this church he'd grown up in. Why in the world would he want to come back here and lead a bunch of people who insisted on reminding him that they'd known him when he was a snot-faced five-year-old who didn't even know how to tie his own shoes? Why did he ever come back to Orchard Grove?

The church was nothing like the one they'd attended when they met. The Long Beach congregation was vibrant, loud, colorful, and outspoken. All kinds of people from all kinds of backgrounds, which made the church potlucks a delectable feast of international flavors. Not like Orchard Grove, where it was casseroles, potato salads, and a few varieties of apple-based desserts, mainly cobblers and pies.

In Long Beach, there truly was a family feel, and the senior pastor had worked there for nearly twenty years. Why couldn't God have called Greg to a congregation like that?

There was one other church in Orchard Grove, where more of the young families went. Sometimes Katrina wondered if she'd even attend Orchard Grove Bible Church if it weren't for the fact that her husband preached here. If they were just a typical newlywed couple, what would they see in a congregation like this?

Even though the Women's Missionary League was quite active, with some sort of fancy event or fundraiser at least once a month, Katrina couldn't point to anybody she truly considered a friend. Joy Holmes was the closest woman here to Katrina's age, but she was so busy with her kids she didn't make it to any of the League functions. It was usually just Katrina and about two dozen women in their sixties and older. Women whose favorite pastimes included commenting on Katrina's fashion style, musical ability, quiet voice, skinny frame, and from now on the topic of her reproductive health would be wide open for everyone to discuss and dissect.

Great.

She picked a spot in the third row. Greg usually wanted her to sit in the front, a fact which she would conveniently forget every few weeks until he reminded her about it. She sat down in the pew, even though most of the congregants were still talking in the back.

Half of them probably about Katrina's miscarriage. She'd never played hooky growing up to get out of school but found herself now praying for a fever or a cough or a migraine that could give her the excuse she needed to leave church and just go home.

Greg was in the front of the sanctuary, talking with two of the elders. He laughed, and Katrina let out her breath. It was about time those men stopped nagging him like they did. They really had no idea how much energy Greg poured out on this little country church. A little country church where half the congregation hated him, and the other half was just waiting for him to do something unforgivable, and all of them were comparing him to other pastors in the congregation's past.

She felt sorry for him. As mad as he made her, as irritated as she got, Greg's job was unreasonably demanding and stressful. With all the strain he was constantly under, it was a miracle they didn't fight even more than they already did.

She drummed her fingers on the church Bible she'd borrowed, the melody from Miles' vocal warmups running through her mind. At least all the talk about the miscarriage had gotten her over whatever guilt-ridden confusion she'd carried into church this morning. She watched her husband, admiring the way his dimple grew so much more pronounced when he gave that genuine smile. With as hard as work was for him, he deserved some more grace. It was hard enough for him to try to become the perfect pastor. He shouldn't also have the burden of being a perfect husband.

Maybe she'd find something special to do for him. She had no idea where the money might come from, but she'd think about it and hopefully come up with a unique idea. Something to let him know she appreciated him.

Something to let him know that in spite of all their stress, she still loved him more than words could ever express.

CHAPTER 31

"You look beautiful today," the old woman said.

Katrina looked over at Grandma Lucy, one of Orchard Grove Bible Church's oldest congregants. Katrina's lilac sweater didn't feel like anything fancy, but it was nice of Grandma Lucy to make the remark. "Thank you."

"Are you saving this for anyone?" Grandma Lucy pointed to the pew and sat down without waiting for an answer. "You're always sitting by yourself Sunday mornings," she remarked. "A pulpit widow." Grandma Lucy reached out her hand and fingered Katrina's wedding band. "This is lovely."

"Thank you."

Katrina hadn't spent too much time with the old woman before. Grandma Lucy came to church with her niece Connie, who was volunteering in the nursery today, but neither of them showed up to any of the League events, as far as Katrina could remember. She wondered how long Grandma Lucy had been here, how many pastors she'd seen come and go, how many pastors' wives had sat here in these pews, alone and isolated.

Pulpit widow.

It wasn't a phrase Katrina would have thought up, but it was unfortunately fitting.

"You look tired, dear," Grandma Lucy observed. "Are you unwell?

Maybe Grandma Lucy didn't have a phone. Maybe she wasn't part of the gossip line also known as the church prayer chain. Maybe she didn't know about the miscarriage.

Katrina offered her best attempt at a smile. "I'm a little tired."

Grandma Lucy nodded. There was something telling, almost sagely, in her expression that reminded Katrina of her voice teacher's frank stares of approval.

Thinking about Miles brought a fresh wave of guilt on top of all the mortification she'd experienced this morning over the miscarriage. *Great.* There was no way she'd be able to focus on her husband's sermon.

Grandma Lucy scooted a little closer in the pew. "You know, I was reading in my Bible this morning, and when I got to Psalm 51, the Lord told me to pray for you."

Katrina had read the Bible, but she wasn't familiar enough with Scripture that she could pinpoint which Psalm was which. She hoped it wasn't one of the angry ones, one of the passages about God's vengeance and anger. She smiled at Grandma Lucy. "Thanks for telling me. "What else was she supposed to say to that?

A few minutes later, when Mrs. Porter's bald and rotund husband went up front and started reading off the church announcements, Katrina opened her church Bible and took a peek. Which Psalm had Grandma Lucy said? Fifty-one?

Have mercy on me, O God, according to your unfailing love; according to your great compassion blot out my transgressions. Wash away all my iniquity and cleanse me from my sin.

Great. Was there anything the people at this church didn't know about? If Nancy had heard Katrina and Miles alone in the sanctuary, who knew what would happen when that gossip started to make its rounds? Katrina could hear the conversations now.

Hello, this is Mrs. Porter calling with a prayer request. Yes, it's about Katrina. Apparently, she was seen in the sanctuary alone with another man. No, not PG. I don't know what it means, and of course we have to be careful not to speculate, but I just felt strongly in my spirit that we should put it on the prayer chain. Ask people to be praying for PG and Katrina and their marriage ...

Snow was falling lightly outside, and Katrina focused on the cascading snowflakes in a vain attempt to get her mind off this congregation, this town, this life. She'd been so excited at the thought of becoming a real pastor's wife at a real church, but now she'd trade in all her titles for the chance to sit in a Sunday service where she was totally anonymous, her life once more totally private, and her secret sorrows and shames were hers to carry alone.

CHAPTER 32

With her husband trying so hard to make everyone at Orchard Grove love him, Katrina still couldn't understand why he refused to preach a traditional Advent sermon series through the month of December. Several of the congregants had already made it known they expected the four weeks leading up to Christmas to be full of nothing but wise men and shepherds and little baby Jesus asleep on the hay.

For some reason, though, Greg had it in that stubborn head of his that a preacher's job was to teach directly out of Scripture regardless of tradition or liturgy or holiday schedules. When the adult Sunday school class made it to the end of Second Corinthians, he moved the very next Sunday to Galatians. In the same way, he refused to stop teaching through First Samuel until he reached the end of the book. Even if you weren't a strict traditionalist like so many folks at Orchard Grove, December was still a strange month for a sermon about Nabal, the fool, and his wife, Abigail (who is either prudent or rebellious depending on which commentator you listen to). Katrina wouldn't tell her husband, but she would have picked the shepherds if the choice were left up to her.

Greg defended Abigail's behavior for the most part, insisting that even though she went behind her husband's back, her actions saved the lives of their entire household. Katrina could never hear a sermon about husbands and wives without thinking about her mother. Divorced twice before finally catching an early Internet entrepreneur who'd already made his multimillions, Katrina's mom was probably the last person worthy of doling out marital advice, even though that did nothing to stop her.

"You need to find a husband who will not only provide for your lifestyle but who will also give you the independence you need." That's what she'd been drilling into Katrina's head from the time she was on husband number two, a plastic surgeon who had no issue sleeping with his patients, whether or not he happened to be married to one of them at the time.

Sometimes Katrina wondered if her mom's biggest problem with Greg wasn't that he was a poor minister but that he would try to control Katrina's life. "I've seen men like him," her mother warned. "Christian men who believe it's their God-given duty to demand nothing but blind allegiance from their wives. He'll have no problem beating you into submission if you show the slightest trace of independent thinking."

Ironic that after two decades of doing nothing but controlling and manipulating Katrina's life, her mom was now all of a sudden concerned about her daughter achieving a healthy sense of independence.

"If you marry that man," she'd said, refusing from the very first day to ever speak his name, "you better pray that he lets you continue playing for the symphony and teaching your lessons, and you better make sure to put that money in your own account under your own name and don't let him touch it. Best if he doesn't even know about it if that's at all possible. That's your only ticket to freedom when you realize that the fairytale you're hoping for is nothing but a lie."

Not exactly the pre-engagement pep talk most girls would expect.

At the time, Katrina had been so in love with Greg, so emboldened by his passion for her, that her mother's words and dire warnings hardly bothered her. And even now that they were married, Greg certainly didn't try to beat her into submission. That was ridiculous. Sure, sometimes he asked her to do things she didn't want to do, like go to the stupid fundraising teas or holiday decorating parties with the Women's Missionary League, but he would never force her to do anything against her will. Katrina didn't have to ask permission or tiptoe around her husband like he was some kind of dictator.

No, that was the way her mother operated. Reading all of her daughter's diaries until Katrina finally developed her own style of cursive scribbles that were entirely indecipherable by anyone but herself. Refusing to let Katrina do anything other than school and music her entire teen years, so that the night she and Greg chaperoned the little dance at the Christian school, it was the very first dance Katrina had ever attended.

Her mom had worried about Greg controlling her life, but really she was just afraid that someone would come and free Katrina from her clutches. Rescue her from her mother's psychotic need to stay in charge of every aspect, every minute detail of Katrina's life.

No matter how hard things got here at Orchard Grove, no matter how bleak the dreary winters and how stressful her position as first lady of this uppity country church, it was still better than the life she'd left. Maybe sometimes it felt like she'd exchanged one form of slavery for another, but she would rather be here with Greg and his stressed-out moodiness than go back and live under her mother's control again.

There were blessings in everything, a purpose for everything. Life wouldn't always be this hard either. Eventually, things would have to get better. She just had to find the patience to wait until then.

CHAPTER 33

Greg ended his sermon at exactly three minutes before noon. The members here were very particular about church dismissing precisely on time, and that was one area where Greg had quickly learned to give in to popular opinion. Not that Katrina would complain. The pews here were probably as old as the church itself, and even though she didn't suffer from backaches or arthritis like so many members here, she was just as ready as anyone else to leave sooner rather than later.

It was snowing again, which meant that Greg would face another afternoon of shoveling and salting the walkways. It would be nice having the house to herself for a little bit so she could sort through some of her emotions. She'd already decided to stop feeling guilty about Miles. She'd done the right thing last night when she asked him to leave, even though her paranoia was unnecessary and that dream she had was just innocuous. First of all, she'd rationalized it during her husband's sermon and came to the firm conclusion that Christians couldn't be held accountable for what their subconscious minds conjured up. Second of all, she was convinced that the dream itself had far more to do with music than anything else. She'd been missing her orchestra friends, longing for the kind of community that can only come when you create such perfect harmonies together. Miles was the first person like that she'd met since arriving here at Orchard Grove, and the intimacy they shared when they made beautiful music together was no different than Katrina working on a duet with her stand partner or practicing with a string quartet. The subconscious mind could be mysterious and bizarre at times, and there was no reason for her to give any more thought to that ridiculous dream.

Greg was about to dismiss everyone when the old woman sitting beside Katrina stood up. "Pastor Greg?" Her voice warbled with age. "Pastor Greg?"

If her husband was surprised to be addressed like that from some strange granny in the pews, he didn't show it. Stepping out from behind the pulpit, he leaned toward Grandma Lucy and asked, "What can I do for you today?"

"I'd like to close the sermon with a word of prayer if I may." It was an odd request, but as long as church got dismissed one way or another, Katrina didn't care who gave the closing. Greg apparently felt the same and handed the microphone to Grandma Lucy without another thought.

"Thank you." Grandma Lucy turned around to face the congregation, her glance landing on Katrina for a full second. What did that look mean? Katrina thought about the Bible passage she had shared with her earlier.

Why would an old woman read a psalm of repentance and think about Katrina?

"I want to close us today with a blessing from the book of Isaiah." Grandma Lucy spoke slowly, and Katrina thought she gained a better understanding of what it would feel like to be a cellist playing the infinite loop that was Pachelbel's *Cannon.*

"*Comfort, comfort my people, says your God. Speak tenderly to Jerusalem, and proclaim to her that her hard service has been completed, that her sin has been paid for, that she has received from the Lord's hand double for all her sins.*" There she went again, harping on sin. And why did her gaze keep landing on Katrina?

"*He tends his flock like a shepherd: He gathers the lambs in his arms and carries them close to his heart; he gently leads those that have young.*" What, was she going to recite the entire book of Isaiah before letting church out? What had Greg been thinking giving her that microphone? The few congregants Katrina could see out of the corner of her eye fidgeted in their pews. Didn't Grandma Lucy realize how highly irregular this sort of behavior was? Or maybe she didn't care.

"The Lord takes such great delight in you." It was a nice thought, but it wouldn't get Katrina out of this service any faster. She'd already planned her escape route, the path back to the parsonage that would hopefully involve the least number of awkward exchanges with women who knew about her miscarriage and had all kinds of unhelpful advice to offer.

"He rejoices over you with his singing." Something in the way Grandma Lucy spoke the words made Katrina stop. *He rejoices over you with his singing.* She'd already resolved to forget about Miles, their awkward meeting last night in the sanctuary, the far more awkward dream she'd had. So why was her brain fixating on this verse?

"He rejoices over you with his singing," Grandma Lucy repeated, "like a bridegroom rejoices over his bride."

Without meaning to, Katrina glanced at her husband, who stood beside Grandma Lucy looking awkward, out of place, and more than a little bewildered. She wanted him to look at her too. Wanted to see in his eyes the same spark, the same passion and love that had first drawn them together. It was hard to believe they'd only been married half a year. It felt more like half a lifetime, like all the mundane worries of life had already sucked away their delight in one another.

Like a bridegroom rejoices over his bride. Katrina had

never liked those Bible passages that compared the church to Christ's bride or anything like that, probably because she'd inherited such a skewed view of marriage to begin with from her mother. It wasn't until she started dating Greg that the verses started to make sense. And that phase had lasted all of a few weeks so that now the most *delight* either of them took in their marriage was when they could go to bed and fall asleep without breaking into some sort of argument.

Maybe her mom was right. Maybe Katrina was wrong to expect anything different. Maybe the fairytale really was a lie after all.

CHAPTER 34

Ten minutes after noon, and Grandma Lucy still hadn't relinquished the microphone or shown any sign that her prayer and Scripture recitation would be winding down soon.

"A voice of one crying in the wilderness." She raised her hand toward the looming fans that hung from the sanctuary ceiling. *"Weeping and great mourning. The voice of a mother weeping for her child."*

Katrina's abdominal muscles seized up. She clenched her hands into fists. Is that what this whole thing was about? First verses that did nothing but remind Katrina how disappointed she was in her own marriage. Now Grandma Lucy was going to poke holes in her already wounded soul and start talking about the miscarriage?

Her heart was racing. She stared at her husband, praying Greg would glance over and see just how uncomfortable she was. He was only a few feet away. Was he so concerned about what people would think of him giving Grandma Lucy the microphone that he couldn't understand how wretched this old woman was making his own wife feel?

"Refusing to be comforted because her children are no more." How was any of this helpful? How was any of this meant to be an encouragement?

Yes, lady, I know my kid's gone. I know I'm never going to see them again. Why do you have to remind me?

It wasn't fair. Katrina had just gotten to the point where she could make music again after all that had happened. She was just starting to heal, getting to the point where her dead child wasn't the first thing on her mind when she woke up and the last image she thought of when she went to sleep. And not only was her health history plastered all over Orchard Grove, some type of current event half the orchardists and their wives would be discussing over Sunday lunch, but now she had to sit through some Bible recitation contest with an old woman who seemed to divine every single struggle going on in Katrina's soul and felt the need to broadcast her inner thoughts to the entire congregation.

As if they needed any more reason to gossip about her.

Next thing, Grandma Lucy would be preaching about the dangers of letting single men into the sanctuary when you're at the church alone at night practicing your music.

It was too much. She couldn't sit through any more. She didn't care how rude it would be or how embarrassing. She'd stand up and yank that microphone out of the old woman's hands if she had to.

Anything to get her to stop talking.

Anything to get her to shut up.

She had just resolved to make her move when Grandma Lucy stopped. Handed the microphone back with a somewhat subdued, "Thank you, Pastor Greg."

Finally. Katrina let out her breath. Her husband mumbled some sort of final dismissal, thus bringing an end to the longest church service in Katrina's working memory.

At least it was over.

She had to make her way past Grandma Lucy to beat the throng to the foyer, so she offered a quick "Excuse me" and tried to slip by unobtrusively.

"Hold on." Grandma Lucy grabbed her wrist. Her hand was softer than Katrina would have thought given all those wrinkles, her grip far stronger than her age might imply. "I'd like to say a prayer for you."

As if she hadn't already said enough. Katrina looked around for Greg, who was fielding questions from two of the elders. There was no rescue. Why couldn't she just tell this woman she had to go home? Why couldn't she simply offer a polite *no thank you* and have that be good enough?

Where was Katrina's voice when she needed it?

Grandma Lucy took both Katrina's hands in hers and, in a voice that was certain to carry over half of the conversations floating around the sanctuary, began to pray.

"Dear Lord, you know this sister's needs. You know her sorrows, her trials, and her joys. I thank you so much for bringing her and her husband here to minister to us at this church. I thank you for her sweet spirit, her loving disposition, her gracious ways. And I pray that whatever longings lie hidden in the base of her soul would be exposed before you. You are good, dear Lord, and we give you praise and glory. Amen."

It was considerably shorter than what Katrina had expected given Grandma Lucy's most recent performance. She accepted the old woman's hug, eyed the path that would take her out of the sanctuary while avoiding as many League women as possible, and longed for the safety and shelter of home.

CHAPTER 35

"You left church early."

It was nearly one o'clock when Greg got home, thankfully this time without company trailing behind him.

Katrina looked up from her pot of soup and scoured his expression for traces of disappointment or anger.

"Sorry about that. I wasn't feeling well."

He slipped off his boots and draped his coat over the back of one of the dining room chairs. "That's fine. I would have left right away too if I could have gotten away with it." He smiled. A tired smile, not at all like the charming, joyful grins he'd lavished on her when they were dating, but at least he wasn't upset that she'd come home right away.

"Some service closing, huh?"

Again, she searched his expression, trying to figure out what he wanted her to say. Was he just making conversation? Or did he somehow suspect that Grandma Lucy had been speaking directly to Katrina?

"It was interesting," she offered, still unable to guess the response he expected.

He stepped into the kitchen and kissed her cheek. "What are you making? It smells good."

"Just some chicken soup." It was canned, but she tried her best to get creative by adding some frozen vegetables and a few spices. There was some seashell pasta in the cupboard she thought about adding, but she wasn't sure if she should cook it first and then throw it in or if she could just dump it in the soup raw and wait for it to get soft.

He slipped his arm around Katrina's waist. She smiled but kept her eyes on the pan. With her luck, if she looked away for even half a minute, it would boil over or start to scald.

"You looked pretty today. I like that purple sweater." He ran his hands up and down her side and hip.

"Thanks."

"What'd you think of church? Did you like the sermon?"

How was she supposed to answer? Was she supposed to admit she'd been daydreaming the whole time? And she still had no idea what she thought about Grandma Lucy or that bizarre closing prayer. She offered a noncommittal response, hoping he wouldn't press her further.

Once the soup was served, she sat across from her husband at the table. He looked more at peace than he had in months. After a quick, somewhat standard prayer for the meal, he raised his eyes to hers. "Everything ok?"

"Yeah." The flush crept up to her face. It was such a juvenile reaction, one she hated about herself.

"Why do you keep staring at me like that?" He grinned, and this time it was easy to guess what sort of reply he was hoping for.

She didn't want him to misread her intentions. "I don't know. You look happy."

It sounded so lame, and she realized that if he wanted to, he could turn her statement around and get mad at her for insinuating he was sad or grumpy all the time. Instead, he wiped his mouth with his napkin and said, "Yeah. It's been a good day."

That was a change. Most Sundays Greg came home emotionally exhausted after getting berated by one or more of his congregants who thought it was their God-given duty to point out all their pastor's faults. *In love,* of course. It was always *in love.*

They ate for a few minutes in silence. Katrina wasn't sure what to do next. Was there something she was supposed to ask to get her husband to explain any particular change in his demeanor, or was this just some sort of fluke? People have bad days for no real reason. Can't they be happy for the same?

"What'd you think of what Grandma Lucy said?" Greg finally asked.

"Which part?" She hadn't meant to sound sarcastic, but the old woman had recited so many different Bible passages and doled out so many random musings it was hard to guess what specifically Greg was talking about. Again she searched his face, hunting for clues that could tell her how he wanted her to respond.

He set down his spoon. "For me, the part that really stood out was about the mother, the one refusing to be comforted." He lowered his voice as if his words were physically dangerous and not to be trusted. "Because of what happened to her child."

Katrina nodded. So her husband was astute enough to make the connection between what Grandma Lucy said and the miscarriage. Was this the part where he'd apologize for the way the women had surrounded her this morning, for the way her secret had slipped its way out into public knowledge across Orchard Grove?

Greg reached out and laid his hand on Katrina's knee. "I don't know what it was about that passage. It's pretty depressing, to be honest, but something about it spoke to me. About the baby we lost. You remember when God took David and Bathsheba's baby? And David said, *I will go to him, but he will not return to me.* I hadn't thought about it in those terms before today, but I really had this sense God was speaking to me about our child. And how even though we lost him, we'll be reunited again in heaven."

Katrina blinked at her husband. Up until now, she hadn't realized Greg thought about the miscarriage anymore.

He offered a boyish shrug. She couldn't remember the last time she'd seen him looking so open. So vulnerable. He gave her leg a squeeze. "I guess God used her words to help me find some closure after all we went through."

Closure. How long had Katrina been chasing for something that intangible? Except she thought she'd been alone in her quest to find it. She'd resented her husband, assuming that he'd stopped mourning when in reality, he'd been grieving too. Only differently.

When had she turned into such a cold spouse? Why had she left him alone with his sorrow? Why had she allowed these barriers to come up between them, pulling them apart at a time when they needed each other the most?

Honesty. That's what they needed. Honesty and vulnerability. When had she stopped sharing her feelings with her husband? When had she closed herself off to the strength and love he could provide?

Maybe if she hadn't, she wouldn't have ended up so

vulnerable, to the point where her subconscious began replacing Greg with someone else, someone who seemed to promise a sense of intimacy she'd been longing for from her husband.

Honesty. It all came down to that, didn't it?

Realizing that there was a chance she was about to make the biggest mistake in her married life, she sucked in her breath, remembered Grandma Lucy's words from Psalm 51 that had spoken so clearly about repentance and forgiveness, and said in the most confident voice she could muster, "I'm really glad you said that, because there's something I have to tell you too."

CHAPTER 36

If the past twenty minutes were the most painfully embarrassing in her entire marriage, it was worth it for this. This sense of comfort, this intimacy she'd been craving.

The lunch dishes remained on the table, the leftover soup cooling in the pan on the stovetop, but she and Greg were together, enjoying each other's presence, relishing the fact that things had finally slowed down enough that they could take this Sunday afternoon nap together.

Or afternoon cuddle, to be more accurate.

She'd told him about Miles. Not everything. Certainly not about the dream, but about how she was starting to feel uncomfortable spending so much time with him. She started off saying she wasn't sure how appropriate it would be for them to meet in the school now that all the students were on Christmas break and there wouldn't be anyone else around.

At first, Greg had shrugged off her arguments. "You're both adults," he'd said, "and you know you have my full trust."

She decided to take it from a slightly different angle.

"Yeah, but don't you think it could potentially make things weird with certain people at the church? If they saw us meeting together every day in an empty school?"

"I guess you're right." That's when he'd leaned over and kissed her. "Have I told you lately that I'm the luckiest man in the world? Thank you for being so honest with me."

The words had sent a twinge of guilt pulsing through her chest. Yes, she'd been honest, but not about everything. She hadn't mentioned Miles stopping over last night while she was practicing at the church, and she hadn't been able to find the words to explain to Greg the emotional connection she'd felt when he helped her discover her voice. But it was a start. Every step forward had to begin with just that. A single step. At least this time, they were moving in the right direction.

She hadn't known what to expect when she opened up to Greg. Her mom had spent so many months doing her best to convince Katrina that she was marrying a jealous, maniacal control freak, one who wouldn't let her have any relationships outside of their marriage, who would throw a temper tantrum any time Katrina tried to do something remotely independent.

Well, her mom had been wrong. Greg wasn't doing anything to keep Katrina locked up. As she lay next to her husband, feeling closer to him and more relaxed than she had in months, she was certain she'd done the right thing by telling Greg what she had.

"What are you thinking about, Mouse?" He asked as he stroked the top of her head.

"Just trying to figure out how to put the lessons on hold without it coming across as awkward."

Greg rolled onto his side and faced her. "You know, I've been thinking. Since you're not comfortable meeting him at the school, why don't you have your lessons over at the church?"

"Really? You think that would be ok?"

"Yeah. Since you're worried about keeping up proper appearances, I'll just make sure that I don't have any meetings or visits scheduled anywhere else so I can be sure to be there while you meet."

"I guess that could work out pretty well," she said, testing the idea out.

She was glad when he changed subjects.

"So I hear that Mrs. Porter volunteered to take over the pageant."

There was so much that could be said in response. She could tell her husband about the overheard conversation in the bathroom, about how she felt equally relieved and dismissed to no longer be in charge of the Christmas pageant. How she wished the people in their church would understand she had no leadership abilities whatsoever. Instead she just rested against his shoulder, so close she could hear his heartbeat. The warmth of their bodies pressed together and covered by the heavy quilts on the bed made her feel cozy and warm in a house that was usually as frigid as Vivaldi's *Winter*. While there certainly was a time and place for brutally honest and deep, heartfelt conversations, there was also a time for silent togetherness, basking in one another's nearness.

Katrina didn't want to break the spell the silence cast over them, and soon she was asleep.

CHAPTER 37

Katrina woke up less than half an hour later. Was that someone knocking?

She'd taken off most of her clothes and did her best to ignore the cold while she threw on a pair of leggings and one of Greg's sweatshirts.

The pounding on the door persisted. Another disadvantage of living in the parsonage since parishioners thought they had an open invitation to swing by anytime, night or day. Oh, well. It's not like two o'clock in the afternoon was an unreasonable time for a visit.

Certain she must look as groggy and unkempt as she felt, she ignored her reflection in the bedroom mirror and hurried to meet her visitor. Hoping it wasn't somebody here to complain that Greg hadn't shoveled the snow yet, she made sure to have a ready excuse just in case and opened the door.

"Mrs. Porter?"

The unexpected guest stepped through the entryway, shutting the door behind her and stamping snow off her boots. "I'm sorry to swing by unannounced," she proclaimed as she took off her shoes and gestured to the living room. "Let's talk on the couch."

Katrina had never been invited to take a seat in her own home before, but she submissively followed while Mrs. Porter led the way to the living room. It wasn't nearly as tidy as she would have made it if she'd known about this visit, but at least there was no dirty laundry strewn about. There was something to be said about small victories.

Mrs. Porter adjusted herself comfortably in Greg's recliner, and Katrina took the loveseat.

"I just had to stop by and get a few things off my chest."

For a violinist, it was an asset to be so connected to your emotions, to be able to experience a wide range of feelings and convey them to those around you. As a pastor's wife, however, seated across from someone as formidable as Mrs. Porter, Katrina's propensity to wear her heart on her sleeve was most definitely a curse. Praying she didn't look as terrified as she felt, she waited silently.

Mrs. Porter spoke animatedly, the many jewels on her fingers casting distracting lights around the room. "I just couldn't stop thinking about Grandma Lucy's prayer this afternoon. You know, most of the time I think that woman's a mile off her rocker, and I'm not ashamed to go on record saying so. She's a believer just like you and me, and if God can use a donkey to get his messages across, I'm sure he can use a woman like that in spite of her eccentricities."

Katrina wasn't sure if Grandma Lucy would laugh or be offended at Mrs. Porter comparing her to a barnyard animal, but she held her peace and waited to hear what she'd come here to say.

"What I started to realize the more I thought about it," she went on, "was that Grandma Lucy was talking to you. That mother mourning because her children were no more. She was talking about you, and I started to think about that conversation we had downstairs in the nursery last week, and there I was making assumptions about your pregnancy, and it turns out I was right, but of course I had no clue that you lost your poor baby, and so I came over here under conviction from the Holy Spirit to apologize."

Katrina blinked, not quite certain that she could trust her ears at this moment in time.

"Here at Orchard Grove Bible," Mrs. Porter went on, "we're all like a big family, you know, just like the Bible says. If one part suffers, all the parts suffer with it. And I just can't tell you how sorry I am for what you and Pastor Greg went through. A miscarriage is a sorrowful thing, especially when it's your first. If I had known or even suspected what had happened, I wouldn't have made such a nuisance of myself last week when we spoke. I hope you believe me, and I hope you'll do me the honor of accepting my apology. It's nothing too flowery, but it does come from the heart."

"Yes, of course." Katrina wondered if that strength and boldness she'd found in her singing would ever work its way into her speaking voice as well.

Mrs. Porter reached into her coat pocket. "Well then, with that out of the way ..."

"Mouse!" Greg's voice was both groggy and playful as he called from down the hall. "Mouse, why'd you up and leave me all alone? It's cold in here, and this bed's far too big for one person all by himself. Don't make me come out there and teach you a lesson."

The bedroom door opened. Katrina jumped from her chair and hurried down the hall, hoping to intercept her husband in time.

No such luck. Out he came, wearing nothing but candy cane boxers and a giant grin that disappeared as soon as he noticed Mrs. Porter in the living room.

Katrina did her best to shield her husband, a difficult task seeing how much larger he was than she.

"Why didn't you tell me someone was here?" he asked through gritted teeth and hurried back into the bedroom.

She followed him in. "I'm sorry. I'll take care of this, you just stay in there," Katrina told him, wondering what in the world she was supposed to say to Mrs. Porter after something like this.

"Well of course I'm staying in here." Greg shut the door on her, and Katrina raced down the hall, a dozen apologies ready to tumble out one after the other, but she stopped when she saw Mrs. Porter's face lit up in silent laughter.

"I'm sorry, dear." Mrs. Proter shook her head. "I should have known. Sunday afternoon, no meetings on the schedule, a young wife as pretty and eager to please as you. It's no wonder Pastor Greg would only have one thing on his mind on a day like this."

This time, Katrina felt certain that not even a classically trained actress could keep herself from blushing. "It's not like that," she stammered.

Mrs. Porter waved her hand dismissively. "Of course it is, dear, and that's just fine with me. You and Pastor Greg go enjoy each other. And now that I know you two are open to the idea of pregnancy, if nobody's mentioned it yet, I may as well be the first to drop the hint that the church is known to raise the pastor's salary if his wife delivers a healthy baby. It's our number one plan for church growth." She laughed coarsely.

"Well, I don't want to make you keep your husband

waiting, not if he's anything like Mr. Porter was at that age." Mrs. Porter stood with another loud, somewhat boorish chuckle. "Oh, before I forget." She reached into her coat pocket. "This is my Christmas present for you. I don't know if you've been to the Safe Anchorage Gift Shop yet, but they have all kinds of candles and lotions and skin products made from goat's milk. Some handmade jewelry and cards and things too if you're into that sort of stuff." She handed Katrina a small envelope. "Now don't bother seeing me out. I know where the door is."

Katrina still hadn't moved from her spot when Mrs. Porter looked back once and winked. "You kids have a fun afternoon. I'll be praying for good news from the two of you before very long."

CHAPTER 38

"No, I will not calm down," Katrina insisted, insulted that her husband would even make the suggestion. "Do you have any idea how humiliating it is to have to listen to someone else talk about your love life?"

Greg hadn't stopped grinning since Katrina came into the bedroom. "Do you have any idea how humiliating it is to come out of the bedroom in your boxers and find that your wife is sitting out there gabbing with the longest-standing elder's wife?"

Katrina shook her head. All she wanted to do was bury herself under the covers and pretend like the past fifteen minutes had never happened, but it seemed like Greg was willing to go to just about any limit to keep her from forgetting.

"What business is it of hers what we do in our own time anyway? And after coming over to apologize for being insensitive about the miscarriage, how the world could she think there is anything justified in what she said?"

"Mrs. Porter was born a busybody and will die a busybody. You can't let her get to you. That's my secret for dealing with half the congregation here, Mouse."

Greg pointed to the envelope Katrina had tossed on the bed. "What's that?"

"Some gift card. Do you know of a Safe Anchorage Gift Shop somewhere around town?"

He nodded. "Yeah, that's where Grandma Lucy lives. Her niece runs the place now. Big goat farm. We took field trips there when I was a kid. So Mrs. Porter gave you a gift certificate to the shop there?" He opened up the envelope and showed Katrina the amount. "Wow, that's generous. Did you know it was this much?"

She shook her head. If Mrs. Porter was trying to pay Katrina off for all the inappropriate comments she'd made, the total would come to a whole lot more than that.

"I'm guessing that what happened has basically destroyed our shot at romance for now," Greg said. "Am I right?"

Katrina pretended not to hear, hoping that her silence would serve as a sufficient answer.

Greg reached out and tossed over her lilac sweater. "Here, put this on."

"Why?"

"Mostly because I like to watch you get dressed. But also because we're going out. You just got an early Christmas present. Time to choose something extra nice for you. Maybe it will be enough to get your mind off of silly old ladies who have nothing better to do with their time than make my pretty wife blush." He smiled and stroked her cheek. "Just like you're doing now."

He reached down for his shoes, patting her backside as he straightened up.

"Come on, Mouse. Let's get out for a while. You look like you could use some fresh air."

CHAPTER 39

"Well," Greg said as he put the car in reverse, "at least we had a nice drive, right?"

"That's true."

"I should have remembered they'd be closed on Sundays. Now that you know it's here though, you can drive yourself tomorrow during the day, or we could come back and choose your present together tomorrow night. Whichever you want."

"Either way would be fine with me," Katrina answered as Greg began the long descent back down the Safe Anchorage Farm's winding driveway.

"I'm sure either way would be fine with you," he said. "That's not what I asked. I asked what you'd choose."

"And I told you either would be fine." She was glad her husband was still in a good mood or she could see this circular conversation irritating both of them rapidly.

"Why do you do that, Mouse?"

"Do what?"

"Never have an opinion on anything. It happens all the time. Once or twice, it's not a big deal, but I seriously feel like the last time you made a decision entirely on your own was when you agreed to marry me. And ever since then it's like I'm living with nothing but a yes girl."

"You're complaining that I agree with you too much?" What had started out as a fun, spontaneous trip to the gift shop was quickly turning into yet another argument. Oh, well. At least they'd had a happy hour together before it all fell apart again.

"No, I'm complaining because either you don't have a mind of your own to make up or you're so worried about disappointing me that you're afraid to express your opinion. And that's problematic either way you look at it. I know it's probably harder for you because of the way your mom ..."

"My mom has nothing to do with this," Katrina snapped. He wanted her opinion all of a sudden? She'd be happy to give it to him.

"You probably don't want to hear this, but I'm pretty sure you're wrong," Greg went on before she could get another word in on the contrary. "Think about it. What's your biggest complaint about the way your mother raised you? It's that she tried to control everything. She didn't let you make any decisions for yourself, from whom you could or couldn't fall in love with all the way down to your class schedule at the community college. I hate that I even have to say this, but that's not normal, you know. Didn't she call up your conductor once and complain that he was keeping you out too late at rehearsals? That's something you do when your kid's twelve, Mouse, not twenty."

Great. First the run-in with Mrs. Porter and now another argument, this time about her mother. Was it possible for the afternoon to get any worse? She crossed her arms, hoping that her husband would understand from her rigid silence how upset he was making her.

"Growing up the way you did, you never learned how to express yourself. With your mom being the control freak she is, it was safer for you to have no opinion whatsoever. That part's not your fault. I get it. I really do. But what I don't get is why you're still acting like you're being controlled, like you're too afraid to speak your mind. Have I done something to make you feel like you can't share your opinions with me?"

Katrina still couldn't figure out how a conversation about whether she should return to the gift shop alone or with her husband could have devolved into a dissection of every dysfunctional aspect of her childhood.

Greg acted like he wanted to know what was going on in

her mind, but if he had any idea how unhappy she was, if he had any idea how much anger and resentment she'd started to harbor about the petty, judgmental members of their church, if he had any idea how many times she'd asked herself if her mom had been right to warn her away from Greg, he'd understand why so often she chose to remain silent.

He kept one hand on the steering wheel and rested the other on her knee. "Know what? This isn't a conversation we need to have right now. I'm sorry I brought it up. We've had a good afternoon together, and even though the gift shop was closed, that doesn't mean the fun has to end. Did you bring your gloves?"

Katrina reached into her coat pockets. "Yeah. Why?"

Greg smiled, any signs of frustration with her erased from his expression. "I'm not going to tell you now. You'll just have to wait and see."

CHAPTER 40

"I still can't believe that your mom never took you skating. Not even once?"

Katrina dug her hands deep into her pockets, trying in vain to warm them up. "Nope. I think she was afraid I'd fall and break my wrist and have to quit practicing."

Greg shook his head. "Have I told you before your mom's a little intense?"

Katrina tried to laugh, but she was still wary of talking about her mother after the way the conversation had turned on the drive over here. She was only now beginning to realize how many parts of Orchard Grove she still knew nothing about. A goat farm with a gift shop attached, an abandoned parking lot turned into an ice-skating rink. She and Greg had been out here for a quarter of an hour or longer, watching as people skated in circles and figure eights while a more boisterous group played hockey on the opposite side of the makeshift rink.

"How'd they get so much ice out here anyway?" she asked.

"They just hose it down every winter, let the cold do the rest. Want to give it a try?" His smile was nearly irresistible.

"I don't have skates."

He shrugged and pointed to some teenage boys goofing off. "Neither do they. Should we join them?"

Although somewhat tempted by the offer, she shook her head, but he had already grabbed her coat sleeve and was pulling her forward.

"I said I don't want to." It was bad enough trying to walk on the ice in the Walmart parking lot. She did that because if she didn't they wouldn't have groceries for the week. Why would anybody do this sort of thing for fun?

"I'm not taking no for an answer." Greg grabbed both her elbows and dragged her ahead. Even where they had been standing, it was slippery enough that she couldn't find any traction to dig in with her heels and stop her husband.

In spite of how nervous she felt, she let out a giggle. "What are you doing?"

"Enjoying an afternoon out with my wife." He leaned over as if he were about to kiss her in front of everybody. She tried to dodge and ended up landing on the ice.

Greg's eyes widened in concern. "I'm sorry. I didn't mean to do that. Are you all right?"

She checked both her wrists to make sure they hadn't

been injured in the fall. Aside from a bruised and somewhat sore backside, she would be fine. Of course, Greg didn't know that yet, and she had to admit that she enjoyed the worried expression on his face.

He reached his hand down. "Here. Let me help you up. Let's make sure you're ok. Are your wrists all right? Did you hurt them?"

"I'm fine," she answered, trying to keep a straight face, "but that's more than I can say for you." She grabbed his hand and yanked down. He fell on his knees, and the momentum almost set his face flying straight into her chest.

With a laugh, he seized her around the waist, raised himself partially, and buried his cheek into her neck, burrowing to find her most ticklish spot. "So that's how you want to play. Now I get it."

She squealed when his chin dug into her shoulder muscle, and between peals of laughter and her clumsy maneuvers on the ice, she did her best to scoot away from him. Standing up was another matter altogether.

She held up a hand. "Pause. I need a time out."

He was leaning over her, and at first she was afraid he wouldn't stop before bursting into another round of playful tickles.

"Pause." She tried her hardest not to laugh so he'd know

she was serious. "This isn't fair. I can't even stand up to try to run away from you."

Greg's smile was catching. "I know. That's what makes the game so fun." In spite of his teasing tone, he stopped pursuing her and helped her to her feet, keeping one arm around her waist and the other hand supporting her elbow to keep her from falling again. "There. You steady now?"

"Hardly." Katrina looked behind her, surprised to find that they were only a couple feet away from where they began. With as ferociously as she'd been trying to run away from him, she wouldn't have been surprised to find herself in the middle of the rink.

"Ready for round two?" he asked.

"No, give me another minute." She was short of breath. When was the last time she and Greg had laughed like this?

He leaned his ear down toward her playfully. "What's that? I didn't quite hear you. You said you're ready to start again?"

"No," she squealed, but her protest was drowned out when her husband gave a giant roar and lunged toward her. She still wasn't used to moving on the ice, but she managed to get a foot or two away before he grabbed her around the waist, sat down on the ground, and pulled her onto his lap.

Skaters swerved to avoid them while they sat there giggling, and Katrina wondered how much she'd be willing to pay for a chance to bottle up this closeness to guarantee that they'd never let months go by again without sharing in simple joys and healing laughter.

CHAPTER 41

Katrina scooted closer to her husband for warmth. "This is officially the longest I've ever stayed out in the cold."

Greg leaned over and kissed the top of her head. "We'll make a real snow baby out of you yet, my little California girl."

She leaned her head against his chest as they walked along the dried up riverbed. The snow was falling. Greg was at least an hour late from when he should have started the shoveling back home, but she was happy.

They were happy.

"Remember that park near your mom's where we used to have picnics?" Greg asked. "Remember that trail? It sort of reminds me of this."

"Yeah, except right now it's about forty degrees colder than it ever was there."

"That's not what I'm talking about. I mean this. You and me, just walking together. No particular place to go, no real hurry to get there. I miss times like that."

"I do too." She spoke the words so quietly, she wasn't

sure if he heard.

"Maybe we can make this a Sunday afternoon tradition. Coming out here to the trail, walking along the riverbed."

For the first time, Katrina thought she might one day get used to winter weather after all. "I'd like that."

They meandered slowly, the snow crunching beneath their boots. While huddling so closely together was efficient to save body heat, it certainly impaired their speed. She wondered if Greg had forgotten about the shoveling but didn't have the heart to bring it up.

"You know what I love about Orchard Grove?" Greg asked. It was a question Katrina had never considered before. She'd assumed everyone who lived here was out of other options or simply didn't know any better. Was it possible that some folks would voluntarily choose to live in a place like this?

"I love how peaceful it is," he answered. "Back in Long Beach, life was so fast-paced. Everybody racing around, trying to outdo each other in every possible way. Here, it's just people. People content to lead simple, quiet lives, just like Paul talks about in Thessalonians."

Katrina didn't know how to respond. Maybe what she saw as an existence stripped from nearly all chance for creative expression, artistic beauty, or sophisticated culture to others might be a welcome reprieve from the hustle of city life. But she didn't want to ruin the optimistic mood by her pessimism and didn't say anything.

"What about you?" How had she known that question was coming?

"Me what?"

"What do you like most about Orchard Grove?"

Katrina stared around her, at the snow covered rocks lining the old riverbed, the footprints ahead of them of another couple who must have recently walked this trail, at the snow that was even now falling and covering their tracks.

"I like the days when we have time to spend together. Like this."

"Yeah, it's been pretty busy, hasn't it?"

"Yeah. It has."

Silence settled around them like the peaceful blanket of snow that covered over all the trash in the riverbed. It didn't clear up the litter, just removed it from sight long enough to give the illusion of true pristine beauty.

Beauty so poignant that if you focused on it one certain way, you could almost make yourself forget the garbage that was buried beneath the surface.

CHAPTER 42

Dinner that night was reheated spaghetti, and Katrina did her best to hide her disappointment that they didn't have a more special way to end their perfect afternoon together.

After walking for nearly an hour through the woods, they finally came home so Greg could shovel and Katrina could try to thaw out her frozen limbs in a hot bath.

"Want to watch a movie after we eat?" It was probably Greg's way of telling her he was in the mood for some kind of action flick with lots of guns and car chases. Definitely not the way Katrina would have chosen to conclude the evening, but she stared at her plate and nodded.

"Sure. That's a good idea."

"I'm not sure we've spent this much time together since we moved here. We may have just set ourselves a record."

Katrina matched his smile. It really had been the perfect day, or nearly perfect at least. She could have done without the part where Mrs. Porter walked in on her husband in his underwear, but she figured that it was something they could laugh about one day.

Especially now that she could remember how nice it was to actually laugh.

"How's your tailbone?" Greg asked. "Does it still hurt?"

"No. I'd forgotten about it."

"What about a bruise? Do you need me to check for you?" His eyes twinkled.

"Maybe later," she answered, trying to match his playful tone.

Greg reached over and poured himself more water. "What do you have going on this week? Anything out of the ordinary?"

She wasn't ready to think about another week. She was too busy relaxing after such a peaceful day. "Not too much. I'll have to call and see about moving my voice lessons to the church."

If the choice had been up to her, she would have come up with some excuse to stop seeing Miles completely, but there was no simple way to do that without owing her husband a lengthy explanation. She'd spent all afternoon trying to forget about her voice teacher and the awkward conversation she'd have to initiate with him. Why couldn't she be more like Greg? He never second-guessed anything. If he wanted to change a meeting place, he changed the meeting place. That's all there was to it. Katrina had to psych herself up for hours just to get to the point where she could make a simple phone call.

"So when do I get to hear all the progress you're making, Mouse?"

She froze with her fork poised over her plate. "Huh?"

"When are you going to sing for me? Back in Long Beach when you were taking violin lessons, you were always playing for me. I miss that."

He missed her playing her violin for him? Why didn't he say so months ago when she stopped?

"It's just singing." Why did she feel so flustered? And why did she feel like she had to make excuses?

"I know it's just singing, but you're my wife and an amazingly talented musician, and I hear Miles is quite accomplished too. Mrs. Porter was just telling me that the singing group he takes to state champions has placed first or second every year since he started teaching here. Pretty impressive for a little town like this."

"Yeah." She'd seen some trophies in the music room but had been too busy practicing with Miles to pay much attention. She hadn't known about the Orchard Grove team ranking so high in the state, but she wasn't surprised. Miles was the kind of teacher who could unlock the musical potential of his students. Katrina could teach the basics and give intermediate violinists a regimented program that would help them progress, but it took a special kind of gifting to draw out the passion and potential in others the way Miles could.

She had never seen anyone do with the violin what Miles had done for her voice in so short a time.

"You still didn't answer my question," Greg remarked. "When are you going to sing for me?"

"I don't know. How about next weekend after I've had more lessons?"

Greg stood up. "How about right now?"

CHAPTER 43

"So this is really where you practice?" Greg asked. "I'm surprised you don't get claustrophobic."

They were in the small cry room of the church, where Greg insisted Katrina give him a demonstration of what she'd been learning.

Greg sat down in the rocking chair. "Wait a minute. You don't sway around when you sing as much as you do when you play your violin, do you? Because otherwise I need to go put on some protective gear. It would be hard to explain to the elders how I got a black eye."

He flashed a smile, but Katrina was too nervous to return it. Didn't he know how much she hated to be put on the spot, especially with her music? That's why performing on her violin for the church had been so unbearable, why she'd rather stop playing at all than create music to meet someone else's whim.

"So what are you going to sing for me?" he asked.

"I don't know." Did he think that after a week of lessons

she'd have a full repertoire? "What do you want to hear?"

"Whatever it is that you and your teacher are working on together."

"It's mostly just warmups."

"Warmups? For as long as you two spend together? Got to be doing more than just that."

It was true. They did do more than that. Like talk about their favorite composers, about the most memorable concerts they'd attended, about how woefully deficient Orchard Grove was as a community in promoting the arts.

She was glad her back was turned to her husband. "Do you want me to show you some of my starting exercises?"

He shrugged. "Sure. If that's all you've got."

Ignoring his disappointed tone, she situated herself in front of the piano and played the first cord. She began with a few simple runs, just enough to get her voice prepared. When she was done, she glanced at her husband, trying to gauge his thoughts from his expression.

"That's it? That's really all you've learned?"

Katrina stared at the piano. "Pretty much. Some of them get more complicated, though. The ones you just heard were pretty basic."

"Yeah. So basic that I could find you a free video online that you could practice with ten minutes a day if that's all you're doing. I guess it's a good thing we're not paying the guy out of pocket. How much does he charge for these so-called lessons he gives?"

She fought the urge to defend her teacher. "I don't know. We haven't discussed money."

Greg scoffed. "Well, if he's making a living selling lessons like this, you could do the same thing for half the price and probably end up with a full studio."

"I'm not a voice teacher."

He shrugged. "Apparently it doesn't take much, at least not in this town."

Katrina didn't meet her husband's eyes.

"Oh, come on," he exclaimed. "Don't get all pouty. I have a right to an opinion, don't I?"

She nodded, more than ready for this conversation to end.

"I'm not saying anything against you. I love your voice. I could never understand why you don't use it more. I just don't see how singing a whole bunch of *mah-mah-mah-mah-mah*s all in a row is going to help you lead music at church. I just figured you'd be doing actual songs." He stood up.

"Where are you going?"

"I thought we were going to watch a movie together."

"I think I'll stay here and practice a little more."

He shook his head. "Now you're all upset with me

because I had a simple opinion."

"I never said I was upset with you."

"No, but I know you. I say one thing about your voice lessons, and now you're all hurt like a little mouse who just got its tail stepped on. It makes me feel like I can't say anything to you without you getting all bent out of shape. That's not fair to me."

"Yeah, you're right." She was ready for him to be gone.

"So you're gonna stay here and practice now? All because I ..." He let out a sigh and didn't finish.

Katrina followed him out of the cry room.

"What are you doing?" he asked. "I thought you said you were staying here."

"I need to get my violin from the house."

"So now you're practicing your violin? I thought you were doing your singing scales or whatever those *mah-mah-mah* things are." Since he wouldn't be here at the church to listen to her anyway, did it really matter?

He shook his head, acting as if that one act sapped all his energy. "Never mind. Just remember to lock everything up when you're done. And turn off all the lights."

CHAPTER 44

She would never play in that stupid, cramped cry room again. She was so tired of being afraid of her own voice. She'd wasted enough time here in Orchard Grove feeling shy and inadequate and overlooked. Months trying to accommodate her music to fit others' expectations, and in the end it sucked all of her creative energy dry. She wouldn't let that happen anymore.

No matter what her husband said, no matter what anyone in this church thought, she was a musician. And a really good one. There was no more room for this false modesty, no reason for her to hide her talents or her voice. She was nobody's little mouse.

Standing next to the sanctuary's gaudy Christmas tree, which was covered in so much golden foil and maroon tinsel that it would have stood out in the middle of the Las Vegas strip, she raised her violin and began to play. Back in high school, her teacher had made her memorize all of the Bach cello suites transposed for violin. They weren't technically demanding, which in the end was what made them so difficult to master.

Years later, she could still improve her performance.

Greg had no idea what he was talking about when it came to her voice lessons. How could he, a self-taught guitarist? He couldn't read sheet music, and even though he could stay in key for the most part, that's about all you could say for his singing. What did he know? What right did he have to criticize Katrina's teacher after listening to her sing for a couple minutes?

Her bow grated the strings. Forceful. Angry.

Bach would be appalled.

She let her fingers fly higher up the register, no longer afraid to let the music soar up to the vaulted ceiling of the sanctuary. She moved past Bach and on to Tchaikovsky. Nobody composed better music to play when you were angry than the Russians. Next up Shostakovich with his barking staccato reminiscent of the machine gun bursts and air raids that nearly destroyed his Leningrad home. Katrina played on, pouring out all her frustrations into the music, but instead of running out of energy, it only fueled the intensity of her emotions.

The sanctuary had more space for her to express herself than the cry room, but it was still far from ideal. She hated the tacky Christmas decorations, the fact that anyone could stop by at any time and intrude on her practicing. But where else could she go? If she were to play like this at home, she would feel compelled to self-censor, to tone down the volume, to keep her intensity subdued. That's all she'd done for the past six months since she'd arrived in Orchard Grove, all any of these orchardists and their petty wives expected her to do. In their minds, she was their pastor's wife first and foremost. Her violin playing made for an interesting hobby, just like some people enjoy baking or quilting.

No one here understood that music wasn't just a part of her life. It was the main reason she existed. If she was back in Long Beach and back with her musical family she had grown to love, she wouldn't feel so isolated. So lonely.

This wasn't her home. There was no sense of belonging here. She'd lost track of how many people Greg had invited over for lunch or dinner at the parsonage over the past six months. And who had returned the favor?

Nobody. Not a single one.

Not that there were many people she wanted to spend extra time with. She had never been part of a church that so aggressively and deliberately belittled their pastor. It was the church that was doing this to Greg, the church that kept him busy and frazzled and stressed out so that most days he hardly had time to spare her a single glance.

It was probably even the church's fault that she felt so awkward around Miles. If she wasn't afraid of all the silly gossips, she probably wouldn't have freaked when he stopped by the sanctuary. And if the church had done a better job building up her husband instead of wearing him down, reminding him every single day of the week of the ways he wasn't living up to their expectations, her marriage wouldn't be under so much strain, which was probably what opened her subconscious up to that dream last night.

If she'd had a healthy relationship with her husband from the start, there wouldn't be any room for distractions, no matter how deeply buried they were in her psyche.

It was the church's fault too about the miscarriage. Not the fact that they'd lost the baby. The miscarriage itself was some sort of medical inevitability, no matter how tragic. But if Orchard Grove hadn't been this prone to gossip, she wouldn't have felt so strongly about keeping her secret from everybody. Even her husband. Today was the first time in months they'd discussed the baby they lost.

Katrina thought back to the words of Grandma Lucy's prayer at church. *Weeping and great mourning.*

Nobody had been here to weep with Katrina. Not her husband, who could have shared her sorrow. Not her violin because she'd been bullied by so many different people who assumed they had a right to tell her what to play, when to play it, and how to play it until she kept Dmitry locked up in his case when she needed his comfort the most. If one in four women suffered from miscarriage like the statistics claimed, why had she spent these past months feeling abandoned and alone?

The music poured out of a soul so broken that she didn't even notice her hot and angry tears until one splashed on her violin's polished wood.

Her bow screeched to a halt on its string, and Katrina lowered her instrument to dry him off on her sweater. It wasn't until then that she noticed the white-haired old woman sitting in the back row, staring intently at Katrina.

CHAPTER 45

"I'm sorry if I startled you." Grandma Lucy stood up from her pew and made her way slowly to the front of the sanctuary.

Katrina hadn't invited an audience. Didn't want an audience. But there was something warm in Grandma Lucy's gaze when she said, "I don't have to be a musical genius to recognize the sound of a troubled heart when I hear one." She stared at Katrina, a frank and open gaze that made her wish she were still concealed in the cramped cry room.

"I didn't realize anyone was here."

"I wasn't trying to intrude on your private time. I just stopped over with my niece to drop off some blankets for the women's shelter, and I heard the pain in your song and wanted to come and talk to you." She sat on the step of the stage and beckoned for Katrina to join her. "Now tell me, if the Lord is the source of your hope and joy, why does your music sound so wounded?"

How were you supposed to answer a question like that?

Katrina felt like a small child getting lectured for not

practicing her scales properly. She wanted to find a polite way to end the conversation, but still, just like so many other times, she'd lost her voice.

Grandma Lucy reached out and squeezed Katrina's hand in hers. "The child. It was you who lost the child, wasn't it?"

Katrina nodded, grateful that she had poured out so much of her angst into her music. Without that sort of outlet, she'd be likely to start crying in front of this near stranger.

A stranger who held her hand tightly and refused to let it go.

"You know there's no reason for you to feel guilty. It's nothing that could have been prevented."

Katrina nodded. Still, how was that supposed to offer any comfort? It wouldn't magically make her pregnant again or bring her child back to life.

Grandma Lucy shut her eyes, and her body began to sway slightly. Either that, or Katrina was dizzy from the intensity of her emotions. Playing her violin tonight had been like releasing a dam, all the tension and sorrow and anger and frustration she had kept pent up for the past several months came cascading down around her. She was tired. Too tired to play anymore, but still not ready to go home to face her husband yet.

Which was just as well, since Grandma Lucy apparently

had no plans of allowing her to leave anyway.

"Father God," she began, still squeezing Katrina's hand in hers, "I come before you boldly in Jesus' name asking that you release your precious daughter from these burdens that weigh her down. I ask in Jesus' name that whatever guilt she feels would be conquered by the power of your cross. I pray that the timidity that's been thrust upon her shoulders would be released, that you would birth in her a courage and boldness that she's never known before. I pray that you would straighten her spiritual spine like you did for the crippled woman two thousand years ago, that she would no longer be bent down and hunched over by the weight of her sorrows and insecurities. I speak release over her today. Release from fear. Release from feeling like she's unheard or overlooked. Release from the enemy who has tried to steal her voice from her, who has lied to her and told her that she has no right to speak up and make her opinion known. I pray that she and her new husband would enjoy the harmony that can only come when two people who love each other have submitted their lives thoroughly to you. May she be an encouragement to her husband. May she stand by him through trials and tribulations, and may you sweeten their time together and give them reprieve from these battles they've been fighting."

Grandma Lucy released Katrina's hand, which had started to tremble, and placed both palms on Katrina's abdomen. Even through her sweater the touch was fiery. Powerful.

Grandma Lucy's eyes were shut, and when Katrina glanced at her face, it was lit with a radiance unlike anything she had seen before. It wasn't a halo, but if she had been a painter, it would be the only way she could symbolize the majesty and radiance that shone from her countenance. A smile crept through the myriad wrinkles on the old woman's face as she prayed. "Heavenly Father, powerful healer, you are the God who gives and takes away. And you gave this young mother a child, a child she was never able to hold, but a child that she loves. A child she still mourns even though she tries to be so brave and courageous. We don't know why you chose to take this baby from her and her husband, but we pray that she would not be like the mother who refuses to be comforted, Lord, because your Holy Spirit is the balm of Gilead. Your Holy Spirit covers over our sorrows, works redemption, and heals our wounds. So heal her wounds, dear Lord. Heal my sister's suffering. Look upon her and all she and her husband have endured, restore their joy and love for one another, and may they rest assured that your good plans for them will never fail."

CHAPTER 46

The church was silent once Grandma Lucy left. Katrina gazed around the sanctuary, which seemed so much emptier without the old woman's powerful prayers shattering the darkness. How would it feel to be a believer like Grandma Lucy, someone whose faith was so steadfast that she carried her own power and radiance with her wherever she went?

What would her friends in California think of this old woman, with her eccentric ways and bold faith? There were only a small handful of Christians in the Long Beach Symphony, but even the unbelievers in the group would have to recognize the intensity of Grandma Lucy's soul.

Echoes of the old woman's prayer ran through her mind. *Healed of all her wounds.* What would that even look like? And had Grandma Lucy only been praying about the miscarriage? Or was there more to it than that — Katrina's childhood with a mother who dragged her through three different rounds of unhappy marriages, who insisted on controlling every single aspect of her daughter's life for so many years she hardly knew what it was like to have an opinion of her own. And when she did, she couldn't express it.

Maybe that was what was so compelling about her voice teacher. Miles was so straightforward. So unafraid to speak his mind. It was the same with Greg early on, part of what drew her to him. That confidence.

And now, thanks to the tactless and highly opinionated members of Orchard Grove Bible Church, Greg lived out most days in the shadows, trying to please and accommodate everyone and letting the stress from his job erode his marriage.

But if today were any indication, maybe things would start to get better. The church might always be stressful. Orchard Grove was just that sort of community, and Katrina would be foolish to think that she could hope for any significant change in a congregation like this. But if she and her husband had a strong relationship, if they were able to enjoy every day the kind of closeness they shared together this afternoon, she could endure any number of superfluous business meetings, catty gossips, and petty complaints about her clothes, about her housekeeping skills, about her cooking, about her general inability to be the pastor's wife the members of Orchard Grove Bible Church thought they needed.

Too bad she and Greg had already gotten into another fight tonight, already tarnished the few hours' worth of peace and harmony they'd created earlier. What had it been about anyway? Oh yeah. Her singing warmups. As if there weren't more important things for a couple to get upset over. She still hadn't called Miles, still hadn't asked him to meet her at the church for tomorrow's lesson. Maybe she'd go ahead and continue singing with him at the school. If all Greg was going to do was poke fun at her attempts to improve her voice, she certainly didn't want to practice in the church while he was around.

Katrina wiped the rosin off her strings but hesitated before she tucked Dmitry in for the night. One more song. Snow was falling, each individual flake illuminated by the streetlamp outside. The decorations in the sanctuary reminded her of an arrangement she'd played at a youth group Christmas party several years ago. If she remembered right, that had been the first time Greg ever heard her play.

Mary's Medley, she'd called it. Not a very creative title, but she was proud of the piece itself. A mix of Christmas songs, both old and new, that focused on Jesus's mother. It had been years since she played it, but the substance was in the piece's emotional lyricism, not in its technical demands.

With Dmitry in hand, she walked back up to the stage and stood by the Christmas tree, at a point beneath the vaulted ceiling where the acoustics were a fraction brighter than in other parts of the church.

Mary, did you know? As she played, Katrina found herself wondering if Mary had experienced any miscarriages after the miraculous birth of the Savior. There was so much about this young mother that had been lost to the annals of history. What was it like to hold baby Jesus for the first time?

And now onto *What Child Is This?* after a transition that was as polished as if Katrina had been rehearsing for weeks.

Whom shepherds guard and angels sing. And yet Mary sat quietly, musing on the birth of her precious baby, storing up all these treasures in her heart.

Katrina didn't know what it felt like to hold a newborn child for the first time, but she knew the weight of a mother's empty arms. Knew the heaviness of that pain beneath your rib cage as your soul cries out for the child you've lost.

Next a contemporary song where the scared and overwhelmed teenage mother prays for God to sustain her. It seemed almost sacrilegious to project this amount of uncertainty and timidity on someone as revered as the Virgin Mary, but tonight Katrina experienced a deeper connection to the piece than she ever had before. Her bow was as soft and graceful as the finest of silks. Her body swayed in time with the music as she allowed the melody to wash over her. The comfort and healing that Grandma Lucy prayed over her didn't seem so difficult to obtain. Katrina infused the music with her own fears, her own uncertainties, her own tenuous hopes, adding embellishments she hadn't thought to insert in the original arrangement.

Thwack.

Her D string snapped in the middle of the phrase. She had an extra one in her case, but she refused to stop, still longing to create that perfect sound, the heavenly breath that is the musician's torturous muse.

She improvised for a few more refrains, playing in the higher positions on her G string or transposing up an octave onto A, but when she finished the last verse, she still didn't think she'd done the song justice.

Breath of heaven …

She was only planning to sing softly, hardly more than a hum, just so she could work out a new transition in her mind.

After the first chorus, Katrina tucked her violin under her arm, shut her eyes, and tried to achieve that deep diaphragm breathing Miles had so recently taught her.

Breath of heaven…

It was the first time she sang in the sanctuary instead of letting the four walls of the cry room dampen the sound of her voice. The notes rang out clear and vibrant, rising up to the vaulted ceiling, dancing in the wide open spaces.

Something Miles told her earlier replayed in her mind. "I'm not helping you create a new voice. I'm just showing you how to find the one you've got."

Could it really be true? Had she truly possessed this gift her entire life? Had this voice that rang out now, that sent her spirit soaring heavenward, really belonged to her all this time? It had lain dormant, trapped beneath a heavy weight of fear, bound by chains of insecurity, but now that it was free, Katrina sensed that she would never be the same again.

CHAPTER 47

At last, she opened her eyes, the sound of her voice still ringing around her.

During her life, she had created a set of core musical memories, moments that were forever etched into her mind, both good and bad.

That time she lost her place at her fifth-grade violin recital, only instead of punishing her, her mother told her she should just work harder so the next year the audience would be even more impressed.

Her first experience with musical theater, playing *Bring Him Home* along with her high school's somewhat unlikely choice for Jean Valjean. In a moment of pity, Katrina had decided to pour as much of her soul as she could into the solo, so that even the local arts reporter who reviewed their show recognized that it was the music from the pit and not from the singer that moved nearly half the audience to tears.

Then there was the night before her audition for the Long Beach Symphony when Katrina had run through the Sibelius concerto she had prepared in the privacy of her teacher's studio. "I don't care what happens at your audition," her teacher said. "You've just played with a power and intensity I've never heard from you before, and no matter what happens tomorrow, I'm never going to forget this performance tonight."

Katrina wouldn't forget either, although now she had another memory to add to her mental repertoire. The memory of singing in this empty sanctuary, of discovering that what her mother told her all these years about her voice was a lie.

She stepped down from the stage, the euphoria of her musical high so strong that she didn't notice Greg standing in the back of the room until he spoke.

"I've never heard anything like that."

She stood where she was, blinking at her husband. "How long have you been there?" It was her same old mousy voice that came squeaking out, not the one that had just filled the entire church.

"I got here a few minutes before your string broke." He stepped into the sanctuary, looking almost apologetic. "I honestly had no idea you could sing like that."

She was trembling, although she couldn't explain why. This was her husband. Even if he'd intruded on such a private moment, there was no reason to be nervous or uneasy.

"I didn't know anybody was here. You should have said something."

"I thought about it, but you were in your little music zone. It was more intense than I've ever seen you. An earthquake could have taken down the building, and you would have gone right on singing." He was just a few feet away now, holding out his arms. "But I'm sorry to make you feel self-conscious. I've always known what a gifted violinist you are, but I had no idea you could make your voice do something like that. Where did that come from?" He glanced around the sanctuary as if the answer might be located in the pews.

She didn't know what to say. The last time she had tried to talk to him about her lessons, they ended up fighting.

Greg shrugged. "Well, if your teacher could get you to sound like that, I'll never make fun of those warmups again," He shuffled his weight from one foot to the other and stared at the violin Katrina still held in her arms. "And speaking of the warmups, I'm sorry if I hurt your feelings earlier tonight. I guess what I said about your lessons was a little insensitive."

"It's ok." Katrina replaced her broken string before tucking Dmitry into his velvet bed. Loosening her bow, she hoped her husband wouldn't notice the way her fingers still trembled.

"Well," Greg said, "it's getting late. Are you ready to head home?"

She nodded. After a performance like this, she was emotionally exhausted. Some of her orchestra friends talked about how music filled them up and gave them energy, but in Katrina's case, it was this sense of being completely dried out that let her know she had inserted her entire soul into her music. She didn't argue or protest when Greg took her violin case and slipped his arm around her waist, leaving the echoes of the song she'd created behind.

CHAPTER 48

Katrina hesitated outside the door of her husband's office. She thought he might have heard her entering the church, but he was bent over his desk, probably looking at numbers for the budget he'd have to present at the next elders' meeting.

She cleared her throat. "Hey."

He glanced up just long enough for her to know he'd seen her. "Hey." He scribbled something on a page, then asked, "Is it time for your teacher be here already?"

She spun her ring around her finger. "Well, that's what I wanted to ask you. I tried calling him to see if we could meet here, but I couldn't get through, and his voice mailbox was full." Why did her face feel so hot?

Greg reached for his calculator. "Just go to the school. He's probably expecting you there like normal. I could use some quiet around here while I go over these numbers anyway."

She didn't realize until then that her husband's somewhat distracted response was exactly what she'd been hoping for.

She hurried back home to grab what she'd need for her lesson. After a moment's deliberation, she decided to bring her violin along too.

Ever since last night, she'd been trying to think of a way to tell Miles about her experience singing. By the time she pulled into the school parking lot, she could hardly contain her giddiness. When she saw his truck in front of the building and the light coming from the music room, her pulse raced.

She hurried down the empty hallways, telling herself that she was moving quickly to warm up from the cold. She burst through the door of Miles' room, nearly breathless from her flight.

He'd been stacking up some chairs by the door but paused when she entered.

"You look different."

She froze a few feet away from him. She wasn't sure what might have changed her appearance unless it was the biting cold outside or her brisk walk through the school.

He cocked his head to the side, still staring at her with that frank intensity that made her feel like he could read each and every one of her thoughts. He beckoned her in. "Come on. Over here by the piano. And while you warm up from the cold out there, why don't you tell me why your face is practically glowing."

CHAPTER 49

Katrina had underestimated how cathartic, how freeing it would feel to talk with another musician about her experience last night in the sanctuary. She described it all in detail, leaving out only the part about her husband coming in while she'd been so distracted by her music.

"I wish I could have been a fly on the wall of that church," Miles mused.

They spent the next half hour discussing other performances in their pasts, sharing more of their musical memories. Finally, Miles sighed and lifted the lid of the piano.

"Well, how about we stop talking about music and actually make some?"

She shouldn't be afraid. So why did her core shake at the suggestion? She had to overcome her nerves.

He played his opening run. She could do this. She just had to focus. Shutting her eyes, she pictured the way her breath had felt coming out from her diaphragm last night and did her best to recreate that sensation. Once she found her confidence, the notes came out clear and bright. She hated to think of how many years she had wasted this gift, believing her mother's lie that she was unable to sing. No wonder she'd always kept her voice so breathy and soft. But now that she'd discovered the true power she possessed, she doubted she could mimic her old timid voice if she wanted to.

It was like she was back in fourth grade again, discovering she could make actual music on her violin after years of boring scales and études and incessantly long sessions with different teachers boring into her the importance of proper positioning. But unlike the violin, which had taken her years to appreciate, her voice had progressed in a much shorter time.

Her only regret was that she hadn't believed in herself enough to discover her talent sooner.

Even her orchestra friends back in Long Beach bought into the lie she'd told them. *Kat doesn't sing. Her voice is too quiet.* So strange to think that all it had taken was this one man to unlock the gift she'd been given.

And unlike the violin, which she'd taken for granted for so many years during her childhood, she wasn't going to squander this treasure she'd discovered. She was going to practice, fine-tune, and grow her talent with the determination she'd thrown into her violin for nearly two decades.

If she'd progressed so far with her voice in just a few weeks, imagine what she'd sound like in a year.

The mere thought made her head as light and airy as a piccolo trill.

After he warmed up her voice, Miles asked, "So what happens now?"

"What do you mean?"

He glanced at his watch. "Well, it's been an hour. We could call it a day, or we could do something else."

"Like what?" There was no rush for her to get home. She'd been cleaning all morning, working with the newfound energy she'd gained after last night. Other than one last load she'd have to take out of the dryer, she was caught up with laundry, the carpets were vacuumed, and she even had some chicken breast thawing in the fridge for dinner tonight.

Miles' eyes were so expressive. She knew what he was going to say even before he spoke. "Would you like to show me the song you sang last night?"

"In here?"

He shrugged. "It's just the two of us. But I don't want to pressure you. It's totally your choice."

Her face was warm. She rubbed her sweaty palms on her pants, hoping he wouldn't notice.

"You could start on your violin," he suggested. "You wouldn't even have to sing if it feels too uncomfortable. Want to do it like that?"

She nodded and unzipped her violin case, conscious of his eyes on her movements. While she was bent over her instrument, she cleared her throat awkwardly. "Oh, by the way, I was wondering if for the rest of the week we could meet at the church instead of here." If her musical transformation had been divinely inspired, it would take an even greater miracle to help her to speak from now on without sounding so timid.

She kept her back to him while she tightened her bow.

"Yeah, we could do that. Why? You like the acoustics better?"

It was as good an excuse as any, and better by far than the real reason. "Yeah."

"Sure." He stood behind her now, startling her with the closeness of his voice.

She straightened up. "I'll need a minute to tune." She glanced at the floor. "I broke a string last night."

"Take all the time you need."

"Sorry." Since it wasn't even clear to her what she was apologizing for, it must sound even more obscure to him.

"No problem."

After tuning her instrument, she faced him, her violin hugged against her chest. "So you want to hear the arrangement I made?"

His expression was warm in this otherwise chilly room. "I'd love that."

Instinctively, she took a step back. How many times had her mother warned her that she'd hit someone with that bow of hers with as much as she swayed while playing?

"You ready?"

He nodded. Trying to share some of the confidence that shined from his expression, she lifted her bow then glanced up once more, waiting for him with the same deference she'd show a conductor.

He gave the signal, and she shut her eyes.

What child is this ...

In a way, he'd been right about the acoustics. It was exactly like playing in a school gym here, which made what should have been rich, soulful tones sound far too airy and bright.

She'd have to try harder. Overcompensate until her music was almost broody. Thankfully, when it came to her violin, Katrina had never been one to shrink back from a challenge.

So bring him incense, gold, and myrrh ...

By the time she got to the second verse, her surroundings had disappeared. She could have been playing on the deck of the capsizing Titanic for all the attention she paid to the outside world. There was nothing except Katrina and her violin and the music they created together.

Nothing at all.

Until a deep, resonant voice began to sing along with her instrument.

This, this is Christ the King.

Miles' voice danced in and out of her refrain, piercing any protective layers she'd encased around her heart, shooting straight to the core of her soul and the source of her inspiration. She'd never heard a violin and a voice meld together like this, so seamlessly. The bow that she drew across her strings summoned forth the song that he made until it wasn't even a duet anymore but one single conjoined instrument, her violin and his voice.

And then she felt his hands on hers. He gave her a look, an appeal for permission. Was he asking her to stop playing?

He paused long enough to whisper, "Sing with me," and now he was the one drawing the music from her throat instead of the other way around.

Breath of heaven ...

Unlike last night in the sanctuary, there was no carpet here to dampen the ringing of her voice. No wooden pews to shape the sound. No pulpit or violin to hide behind. Nothing at all.

But she wasn't afraid. While Miles took the lead, she slipped into harmony, which came so naturally to her as a second violinist, and together their voices danced so that it felt as if a conductor was keeping them in unison with his invisible baton.

There were no words to describe the harmony their souls made as their voices united. Previously, Katrina had always believed string quartets to be the most intimate of ensembles, but the closeness shared with three other string players was nothing like this. Singing with Miles, no instruments between them, was complete and total vulnerability. No stands to hide behind, no sheet music to tell you where the song was going next. You had to feel your way, visceral and deep, into the soul of your partner, anticipate his movement, sense his needs, rise up to meet each and every one of his expectations.

They were no longer teacher and student but two hungry souls, yearning together for the beauty their voices and their voices alone could create in a dreary and otherwise lonely universe.

CHAPTER 50

Just like it was impossible to describe the power and passion they'd infused into their music while they were singing together, Katrina couldn't describe the subtle sense of letdown that invaded the space between them when their song was done. Their notes rang out, sharp and shrill, with that tinny echo you get in a gym. It wasn't discordant, but it certainly didn't do justice to the music they'd just created.

Katrina was breathless, but after that sense of intimacy she'd shared with Miles only seconds earlier, it was hard to feel embarrassed. That was one thing you could say about singing compared to playing an instrument. When you relied solely on your voice, every blemish, every imperfection could only come from you. Katrina's singing hadn't been perfect, but it had been more real and open and powerful than any music she'd created in months.

Maybe years.

Which was why she didn't blush but glanced at Miles expectantly. He was the teacher once more, the leader, the only one who could say or do something to summarize the experience they'd just shared.

He stared at her, standing so close she wasn't sure if she could sense the heat in the empty space between them or if that was just her imagination. His chest rose and fell with each breath. She felt her throat constrict for a second, like an aftershock, and she didn't try to speak.

He lifted his hand. Slowly. She couldn't have moved even if she wanted. He reached out, so close to her cheek, then pulled back and rubbed his chin.

"That was great." Now he was the one speaking timidly, giving no indication of the power that had poured out from him.

She wanted him to look up, wanted to sense the approval in his eyes that she'd seen just seconds earlier. She was the child in need of reassurance, the student longing for her teacher's praise.

He cleared his throat. "You should probably rest your voice now. See you."

And he walked out of the music room, his footsteps now the only sound in what had so recently felt like the chamber room of heaven itself.

CHAPTER 51

"You didn't tell me how your lesson went today," Greg commented over dinner. The chicken was too rubbery, but otherwise the meal had turned out well enough.

Katrina didn't know what to say. She'd replayed those last couple minutes in the music room all afternoon. By the time she'd packed up her violin and headed to her car, Miles' truck was gone. She didn't know if she was supposed to do anything to lock up and even waited around a couple extra minutes to see if he'd come back before finally driving home like a puppy who'd just been punished.

"I think my voice is getting a little strained from all the extra practice." She'd made herself two cups of tea with honey already, and her throat still felt raw.

"Well, don't overdo it," Greg told her. "Because I have an idea. That song from last night, the Christmas one, I was thinking maybe you could do it as a solo at the Christmas Eve service."

"You mean on my violin?" She wondered if he

remembered that arrangement, if he recognized it from that youth group party so many years earlier.

"I guess if you wanted to, but I was thinking of you singing it."

She stared at her plate. She'd run out of frozen peas and was forced to heat up the vegetable mix with lima beans, which were bad enough fresh but felt mushy like wet chalk once frozen. "I'll have to think about that."

"No pressure." Greg's voice was tentative, like he was scared she'd be upset.

She offered a smile to make sure he knew there was no reason to worry. "I'll let you know."

He met her smile. "Hey, I found that old guitar book of Christmas carols and was going to spend a little time practicing after dinner. Care to have an old-fashioned singalong?"

A week ago, even a few nights ago, she would have loved the idea. Right now, her soul felt too heavy. "I'm not sure my voice can handle any more singing today," she admitted.

"How about on your violin?"

She loved that he was inviting her to share some time of music together with him. Loved the hopeful earnestness in his expression.

Despised herself for letting him down. "I'm really tired. It's been a long day."

In spite of all the extra cleaning and housework she'd done this morning, in spite of dinner being served on time, Greg hadn't said anything about the added effort. If she weren't so exhausted, it might not matter, but now she felt like she'd wasted all that energy for nothing.

Greg frowned. "Are you all right? You look pale. Do you think you're getting sick?"

"I don't know. Maybe." That could explain the achiness in her bones, the tightness in her throat.

"Why don't you pick a movie instead, and we'll wrap ourselves up on the couch with some blankets and just take it easy?"

She sighed. "No, that's ok. I think I'll just clean up the kitchen and head to bed."

He reached over the table and felt her forehead. "You sure, Mouse?"

She nodded and answered in as clear and definitive a voice as she could, "Positive."

CHAPTER 52

Katrina hadn't taken her eyes off the clock. Ten minutes late. It wasn't that big of a deal. But what if he'd gotten in a car wreck? Snow had fallen last night, and the roads were icy.

She unpacked Dmitry, strummed the strings to make sure he was in tune, and set him back in his case in order to stare at the clock some more.

Where was Miles?

She replayed their conversation yesterday at the school. She'd asked him about meeting here at the church, and he'd said that wouldn't be a problem.

For the past ten minutes, she'd been walking alternatively from the front of the sanctuary to the window overlooking the parking lot. Every so often, she'd take a detour to the cry room and glance at the piano. She should start her warmups, but she didn't want to bother her husband, who was hard at work in his office. Apparently, the previous pastor hadn't created his budget proposal with the right template, so Greg had to toss out all that he'd already worked on and start over again by hand.

The last thing she wanted to do was bother him, but at exactly 3:14, she knocked timidly on his door.

"Come in." His voice was cheerful. Maybe he was expecting someone else.

She nudged the door open and stood at the threshold. His church office was always so intimidating. Expansive shelves lined one full wall and half of another, piled in some spots two or three books deep. Most of the titles had been inherited from previous pastors or donated from the Christian bookstore when it went out of business.

She didn't step in but bit her lip when Greg passed her an impatient glance. "Yeah?"

"My teacher hasn't shown up. I wonder if he's waiting for me at the school." Tucked within the statement, clear from the upward lilt of her voice, was a question. What was she supposed to do now? It was Greg's idea that they move the lessons here. They hadn't discussed what would happen if Miles didn't show.

Greg flipped a page of his budget report with ink-smeared fingers. "So go to the school and find out."

And that was her answer. "Ok." She didn't wait for him to look up, discuss the issue further, or change his mind. She took one tentative step into his formidable workspace, reached for the car keys on the corner of his desk, and made a hasty retreat, careful to shut her husband's door behind her.

CHAPTER 53

There was no reason to be this anxious. What was the big deal? Miles would either be at the school waiting for her, or he wouldn't.

The problem was she wasn't sure which outcome would be worse.

If he was waiting at the school, it might be as simple as him forgetting the conversation they had about switching venues, but with as awkward as it was asking to change plans in the first place, she didn't want to undergo a repeat performance.

But if he wasn't there, what did that mean? That he simply forgot? Was their time together that insignificant? Had she imagined the closeness they felt yesterday, dreamed it all up because she was lonely and pathetic?

Her pulse slowed down when the school parking lot came into view. No truck. No cars. No anybody. Not even tire tracks in the fresh snow.

What now? Should she pull up and wait? Maybe he was late.

In which case he might already be waiting for her at the church.

It's not like she was paying him for his time. Maybe there'd been a misunderstanding. Maybe yesterday had been their last lesson together.

Or maybe he was avoiding her.

It didn't make sense.

She didn't know what to think, and she didn't know what to do. She'd left in such a hurry, her phone was still at home on the kitchen counter. Which was just as well, since she didn't want to call him. There was no way to start a conversation like that without sounding accusatory. *Hey, where are you at? I've been waiting twenty minutes.*

She stopped in the parking lot to think. If she just went home, she could go on with her day. Greg was so busy he wouldn't realize she returned early.

After several minutes with the car heat blasting, the steering wheel was still cold to the touch. In addition to her phone, she'd forgotten her gloves at home too. She always liked to wear them before her lessons so that her hands would take less time to warm up if he wanted her to play her violin.

Which she now remembered was also at the parsonage.

What had happened to her head?

She shoved her hands into her coat. At least while she

decided what to do she didn't have to freeze. That's when she felt the small envelope in her pocket. What was it? Oh, yeah. The gift card from Mrs. Porter. Safe Anchorage was on the outskirts of Orchard Grove, all the way out on Baxter Loop, but it wasn't as if she had anything else to do. And Greg had told her yesterday she could take herself there if she wanted.

Assuming she could find the place again without getting lost.

It shouldn't be too hard. She put the car in reverse and pulled out of the parking lot, ready to leave her disappointment behind.

CHAPTER 54

The Safe Anchorage Gift Shop surpassed Katrina's expectations to the same degree Rachmaninoff's piano concerto surpassed *Chopsticks*. The items in the boutique were as artistic and creative as anything Katrina had seen in Southern California but were sold at half the cost. If she ever started to feel homesick, she could come here.

Colorful earrings made of intricately blown glass beads. Necklaces exquisitely carved from bone or shell. Goat-milk lotions, skin creams, and other health products in packages that were themselves miniature artistic masterpieces.

The graceful hues and subtle scents were like food to Katrina's soul. The paintings on the wall, each one of them originals for sale, ranged from purely abstract splashes of color to realistic pet portrayals or impressionistic images of serene mothers with their children, as graceful as a Viennese waltz.

"May I help you, dear?"

Katrina recognized Connie, Grandma Lucy's niece who

herself was somewhere past middle-aged. Her smile was warm and inviting.

"I'm just looking."

The bells on the front door jingled, and Mrs. Porter's loud exclamations preceded her into the gift shop. "My word, that ice out there is something else. Hello, Connie. Good to see you looking healthy and well today. And Katrina. So you came to spend the money I gave you."

Katrina nodded and picked up the brightly colored scarf she'd been eying.

"Oh, no." Mrs. Porter grabbed the offending piece of cloth and shoved it back on the rack. "That yellow will do nothing but drown out your complexion. It's all wrong. What about this teal?" She held the new scarf up against Katrina's face and asked Connie, "Don't you think this one's a better fit?"

Connie was the kind of woman whose mouth had never learned how to properly frown and whose voice had probably never uttered a sharp word. "It's whichever she feels most comfortable in. Everything here is lovely, if I do say so myself, and she's got one of those figures that can look good in anything."

"It's not her figure I'm worried about," Mrs. Porter explained with a pout. "It's that pale skin." She thumbed through a few more scarves before handing Katrina a lilac one. "Here. Take this. It will go well with that sweater you wore to church Sunday. Although you might want to save it for spring. Maybe it's different in LA, but violet's not really what we'd call a winter color here in Orchard Grove."

Katrina remained speechless as Mrs. Porter turned to another display. "And what about jewelry? Are you looking for earrings today? Something to go with your new scarf? Or what about a necklace?"

Some of the other women in the symphony had learned how to play with bracelets sliding up and down their arms or necklace chains getting stuck beneath their shoulder rests, but Katrina was content with simple earring studs and her plain wedding ring. Leaving Mrs. Porter to eye the jewelry alone, Katrina made her way to the back of the store, where hand-bound journals, painted greeting cards, and small gift books were displayed with an artistic touch. She picked a flowered diary from its shelf.

"That's a new batch we just got in," Connie explained. "Made here locally. In fact, you know her. Joy Holmes from church. Young, pretty mama. Lots of kids. One more on the way you know ..."

From the jewelry section, Mrs. Porter produced a sneeze that was as unconvincing as it was loud. "Oh, Connie!" she called out in a falsetto. "Could you help me? I can't decide which pair of earrings I want to take down to my daughter when we go visit."

Connie bustled over, and Katrina pretended to study the journals while Mrs. Porter conveyed in a whisper that was not nearly as hushed as she probably thought, "You know Katrina's just had a miscarriage, don't you?"

Connie's words were too low to hear, but not Mrs. Porter's response.

"I thought maybe you hadn't heard. It's probably best not to mention Joy or the baby, don't you think?"

Connie coughed awkwardly, and Mrs. Porter announced in a loud, grating voice, "You know, I think you're right. I think she'll like these turquoise ones better. Thanks, Connie. I don't know what I'd do without you."

CHAPTER 55

Katrina returned to the parsonage after leaving the Safe Anchorage Gift Shop empty-handed. The first thing she did was check her phone. No messages.

What happened to Miles?

Maybe she should call. But it was so long after their scheduled lesson time. Why would she try to get a hold of him now? If she wanted to talk, she should have called sooner.

He probably just forgot. A simple mistake, and if she were to ring him up now, it would only make him feel bad.

She'd wait until tomorrow, and if he didn't show up then, she'd force herself to call. Sooner in the day this time so she wasn't left indecisive like this.

Staring at the cluttered kitchen counters, she tried to think of something she could make for dinner. She was out of inspiration, but unfortunately she and Greg had eaten up the last of the leftovers at lunch.

Spaghetti again?

Well, whatever it was would have to wait until after the prayer meeting.

The front door burst open, sending a blast of cold to the base of Katrina's spine. It slammed shut with even more force, rocking the whole house.

"Where are you at?"

He was angry. What had she done or forgotten to do? Did it have anything to do with her music lessons?

"I'm in here," she called out, trying to force cheer into her voice. It was probably something with church. Hadn't he been focused on the budget all day? It was enough to work anyone up into a temper.

He stomped into the kitchen. "We need to talk."

Her heart gave a faint flutter, reminiscent of the closing trill in Stravinsky's *Rite of Spring*.

Trying her best to walk on steady feet, she followed her husband into the dining room. "Is everything ok?"

He scowled without looking at her. "No, everything's not ok. I just spent forty-five minutes tearing apart my office trying to find the receipts for our reimbursement check."

Katrina bit her lip.

Greg continued to glare. "Well?"

"I forgot to copy them." If her voice had been any quieter, she couldn't have heard it herself.

"What?"

She did her best not to flinch at Greg's roar. "I'm sorry." She glanced at the wall calendar hanging in the kitchen, but it was too far away for her to make out the dates.

"You know we need those by the fifteenth. Especially this month with all the extra expenses."

"I know. I'm sorry."

"And we talked about it last week," he added. "I asked you to get them done a few days early since I knew I'd be working on this budget."

"I know. I'm sorry." She sounded like *The Blue Danube*, timidly offering the same two-note phrase over and over.

"Now they're not going to be ready by tomorrow morning when Nancy comes over for the treasurer's meeting, and so we'll have to wait and submit them next month, and that basically eats away half our grocery money and anything extra we wanted to have for Christmas. Plus it messes up the church budget because now some of this year's expenses are going on next year's report."

"Why don't you let me go copy them now real quick? It won't take me long to find them."

"And then what? Huh? Because tonight's the prayer meeting, tomorrow morning is the men's breakfast, and after that I'm going straight back to my office to meet

Nancy, so when am I supposed to fill everything out and get them in on time?"

"You don't have to do anything. I can make the copies and fill out the paperwork now, and you won't have to touch it."

He glowered at the microwave clock. "When? The prayer meeting is about to start. We've got to go open the church up, I need to throw some salt down on the walkways ..."

"Do you want me to get those receipts now or not?" There was no reason for him to yell for ten minutes when it would take her two to find the records he needed and get them over to the church. If he stopped fussing about it and allowed her to focus on her job, everything could be filled out, signed, sealed, and ready before the prayer meeting even started. She could hand them over to Nancy Higgins herself. Greg wouldn't even have to touch the envelope.

"I already told you," he shouted, "there's no time." Which was technically true if he continued to waste precious minutes fuming.

It wasn't his fault. Not all of it. He was under so much stress. All the extra holiday events, the annual budget meeting, their personal finances already as strained as a frayed violin string about to snap.

Anybody in his situation would feel frazzled.

At least that's what she told herself to keep from yelling right back at him.

"What'd you do all day, anyway?" His voice was calmer now, but based on previous experience, she knew that wasn't necessarily a good sign.

"What do you mean?"

"Exactly what it sounds like. I want to know what you did all day."

What did he expect? A minute-by-minute rundown of every single one of her activities since the moment she woke up?

Unfortunately, it was harder to answer his question than it probably should have been. She'd piddled at some housecleaning this morning, put the sheets in the wash but not the dryer. Cleaned and dried one load of dishes, which meant that by now there were two more loads waiting for their turn.

He shook his head without giving her time to respond. "That's what I thought."

"What do you mean? I didn't say anything yet."

"My point exactly." He gestured to the messy counters. "Look around you. What do you see?" He grabbed a dirty pan and held it up. "Because I see dishes all the way from last night that still haven't gotten clean."

"That's not true," she protested. "I washed that one this morning and then used it again for the vegetables at lunch."

"Fine." He set down the pan and picked up one of the large microwavable bowls. "But this is old. See? Here's two lima beans from last night's dinner. And it's still sitting here on the counter. Still taking up space when all you need —" He squirted some soap into the bowl, swirled it around with some running water, and rinsed it out. "— is fifteen seconds to clean it up. And here." He grabbed a towel. "Here's five more seconds to dry it. See? Twenty seconds max. That goes for this pot and these mugs and this bowl of leftover breakfast cereal ..."

"All right." She brought her sweaty hands up to her temples. "I get it. You've made your point."

"Really? Because I'm not sure I have." He stomped into the living room. "What's this? Isn't this the same pile of laundry that was here when we went to bed last night? And here we are almost a full twenty-four hours later, and it's still in this exact same spot? Look at this." He picked up a bra and twirled it around his finger. "What happens when the Porters or the Higginses or anyone else from the church stops by? Hmm? Is this what you want them to be staring at while they're here?" He waved the bra in front of her, and she gave a halfhearted attempt to swat it away from her eyes.

"I'm not trying to be mean, and I'm not trying to complain," he said. "But look at this place. It's unacceptable."

There was no appropriate response. She looked around and realized her husband was right.

"I know it's not fun folding laundry and doing dishes all day, but do you think I'm having a blast pouring over these stupid numbers for that budget meeting?"

"I never said you were," she mumbled.

He went on as if he hadn't heard her. "I don't want to be a demanding husband. I don't think I'm asking too much. A clean house. Not spotless, but clean enough so that if company drops by unannounced — like you know they will — I don't feel like I have to make excuses for my embarrassment of a wife."

Katrina's body tensed while Greg's visibly deflated. "I didn't mean it like that, you know. It's just ..."

His not-quite apology was interrupted by a knock, followed immediately by the sound of someone opening the front door.

"Pastor Greg?"

Katrina was too numb to try to recognize the voice, and she was too tired to think about hiding that bra.

"Pastor Greg? You in there? We were just wondering

if prayer meeting's been cancelled or if you'll be joining us tonight."

He let out his breath. "Yeah," he called out in his cheerful church voice. "I didn't realize it was already that time. We'll be right over."

CHAPTER 56

The last place she wanted to be tonight was at a prayer meeting with her husband, and with as hurt and angry as she was, she probably had solid biblical reasoning to stay home. Didn't Jesus himself say that if your brother had something against you, it was best to go and be reconciled first and then come back to make your offering?

Whoever it was who'd stopped by to find the truant pastor must have heard their arguing. Greg's arguing, to be more precise, since she hadn't raised her voice or said hardly anything. What had they gone back and reported to the congregation? Or how many of them had overheard Greg's yelling as they made their way up the icy walkway to the church? At least the prayer meeting was the most sparsely attended of all the Orchard Grove weekly events.

She had no will to be here, and if you were to take Jesus' words literally, she had no right to be here either. Not when she was so mad at Greg. Just because he was stressed at work, what made him think it was appropriate to take all his frustrations out on her? Just because the congregants at Orchard Grove were mean, spiteful individuals who gossiped about every petty shortcoming they found in their pastor didn't mean that her husband had the right to treat her like rosin dust, something unsightly to be removed as soon as practically possible.

She was reasonable enough to admit that even though he should never have blown up like that, Greg was correct. She'd done a terrible job keeping up the house ever since they got married. Apparently, that's what happens when you grow up in a home with a mother who always hired maids to do the chores.

She wouldn't take responsibility for her husband's juvenile temper tantrum, but she could work harder to stay on top of the housework better. Really, there was no excuse for her behavior. She had all day to get things done. Even her time away from home at the Safe Anchorage Gift Shop had been more about distracting herself from thinking about her music lessons than anything else. She hadn't even left the store with anything to show for the time she wasted there.

It was probably just as well she missed her voice lesson today. After making fun of her warmups, Greg didn't need another reason to hate her teacher.

The first half of these prayer meetings may as well be

rechristened "health updates about every single member of Orchard Grove." If an outsider who had no idea about Christianity walked into the building on a Tuesday night, they would go away feeling like the only reason to join a church was so that if you had an upcoming doctor's visit, there would be at least two dozen people around town who knew about it.

Katrina was sitting in her regular place next to Greg, and she tried to keep her expression neutral. The last thing the prayer chain needed was a request for Pastor Greg and Katrina to have more "unity" in their marriage, which was the code word you used for a couple on the brink of divorce or who had already separated.

Time marched by slowly and arduously, like the unending procession of *Pomp and Circumstance* except in this case there was no majestic finale to look forward to, just the second half of the meeting when everyone took turns telling God what they'd just spent an hour telling each other. Katrina had never been comfortable praying out loud, something that her husband had been arduously trying to change about her since they first arrived in Orchard Grove.

"What kind of message is it sending to people when the pastor's wife doesn't even pray at a prayer meeting?"

He'd asked that dozens of times over the past half a year,

so much so that she'd stopped bothering to explain to him that she prayed just as much as anyone else in attendance, only silently.

It was Greg who began their time of prayer tonight, which was somewhat unusual, given that he preferred to save his thoughts for the closing.

"Dear God, glorious Lord and Savior, King of the universe and sovereign over all creation, we praise you."

When he had been nothing but the youth pastor at the large Long Beach congregation, his prayers had been humble and simple, without these flowery preambles. Yet another way Orchard Grove had corrupted him.

Katrina was glad that her eyes were closed so that no one could see the way they rolled. Was she seriously expected to sit here and listen to her husband pretend to be so righteous and godly less than an hour after he told her that he was embarrassed by her?

Unfortunately, that's exactly what she was expected to do, because she was the first lady of Orchard Grove Bible Church, a role that had at one point sounded so prestigious. Well, if being the pastor's wife meant she had to not only put up with a monster of a husband but pretend along with him that he was some divinely appointed super saint, she wanted no part of it.

It was bad enough that she lived here in this fishbowl of a community, scrutinized by every opinionated member of the Women's Missionary League. She was under enough strain to be perfect from the outside. She didn't need the pressure coming from her own husband as well.

Well, if he was so ashamed of her cleaning abilities, maybe he should try to be the one to keep up all the laundry and the dishes and the tidying. See how well he could manage it. If there was any money to speak of, she would seriously consider flying back to Long Beach. Not necessarily forever, just long enough to fill her soul with those relationships of hers that were actually warm and nonjudgmental. How sad was it that it was her non-Christian friends from the symphony who were far more accepting than her husband and the members of this church?

The biggest problem with returning to Long Beach, aside from the fact that it was financially impossible, was that it would prove her mother right. That alone was enough to dissuade her, but not enough to keep her mind from wondering what it would be like to perform with her friends again. The holiday Pops concert was just in a few more days, and she would miss it because she'd fallen in love with the man who had his heart set on pastoring the most difficult congregation in the Pacific Northwest.

Greg prayed for each and every health request that had been raised earlier, but he still didn't show any signs of slowing down. Maybe after Grandma Lucy's closing last Sunday, he felt the need to reclaim the Orchard Grove record for long-windedness.

"God, we confess our shortcomings to you. Forgive us for those times when we bicker and fight instead of showing grace to one another."

His hand reached over and sought hers out, giving it a gentle squeeze. "Teach us to do a better job loving one another and living in harmony like you want us to. Remind us that love is the greatest gift of all."

It wasn't the heartfelt apology she deserved. It certainly wasn't enough to erase the words her husband had spoken to her, but if previous experience had taught her anything, it was probably all she could expect.

CHAPTER 57

Five minutes after three, and still Miles hadn't shown up to the church for their lesson. Maybe she'd misunderstood. Maybe he was taking the week off because of Christmas, except that didn't make any sense. Wasn't the whole point of taking lessons now because classes were out and he had the extra time?

Well, she wasn't going to waste the gas to drive over to the school a second afternoon in a row.

At least she and Greg had been on better terms. He came home from last night's prayer meeting a little more subdued, a little more reasonable. If only she could live with the man he pretended to be behind the pulpit each Sunday.

But the yelling had stopped. And he'd made more effort than usual at pillow talk, which was also an improvement. It wasn't perfect, but what marriage was? She remembered a lesson he'd taught all the way back during her high-school days in his youth group. *Change the things you can change, then thank God for the things you can't.* It was simple and trite, but there was some truth to it. There was no magic formula that would transform her husband into the loving, caring, sensitive man she wanted him to be. She just had to make the best of what life had given her and do so in a way that didn't leave her bitter.

That was her biggest struggle right now. She'd been convicted at last night's prayer meeting about how resentful she'd grown, not only of her husband but of the people in Orchard Grove. Even if Greg's position here was far more stressful than either of them could have anticipated, it wasn't fair to blame the church for their marriage problems. Every couple had to learn to cope with stress. You couldn't live your whole life in a honeymoon, avoiding anything remotely upsetting.

Like the miscarriage. So many of their problems had started last October, when Katrina was mourning by herself, unable to talk to her husband, unwilling to share her sorrows with the members of her church. As easy as it might be to villainize Greg and the people he worked for, she was far from flawless herself.

She'd confessed her bitterness and resentment to God at the prayer meeting last night, then came home and continued praying before Greg came to join her in bed. Once she started dwelling on her sins, once she really started to see herself as

God did, she wondered if she'd ever reach the end of her list of faults.

Bitterness toward her husband. Bitterness toward nearly every member of his church. Resentment over the way she and Greg had been treated. Anger over the miscarriage. Laziness that kept her house in such a deplorable state her husband was embarrassed. Unforgiveness over the way he insisted on pointing out her faults.

The problem with sins was they were like dirty dishes. No matter how many you confessed, there were still more to be forgiven for the next day. Katrina had started the morning after the prayer meeting grumpy, and it was actually Greg who'd tried to cheer her up while he got dressed for the day. His jokes were even cornier than normal, and his attempt at humor did nothing to heal the wounds his words had inflicted when they fought last night, but at least he was making the effort.

Which was more than Katrina could say about herself.

Once he left for the men's breakfast, she resolved to be productive around the house, reminding herself that things could be so much worse.

At least she didn't have her mom breathing down her neck every minute of the day. Orchard Grove, as flawed as it might be, was still better than life under her mother. Being told what to wear, having every outfit and piece of jewelry pre-selected and pre-approved. Being kept at home so she wouldn't get sick before a big audition, prevented from having any fun because she might fall and break her wrist. At certain points during her teen years, Katrina had daydreamed about smashing one of her fingers on purpose just to spite her mother.

It was never a good idea to spend this much time dwelling on the past. Katrina looked up at the sanctuary clock. No Miles this time either. She'd go home and give him a ring. As much as she hated to do it, she might as well stop wasting time waiting for a lesson that wasn't going to take place. Besides, her fear of making a simple phone call was petty and immature, just like so many other things about her.

She hadn't even bothered bringing Dmitry over to the church, guessing that the afternoon would turn out the way it did. She stopped by Greg's office on her way out and gave a little knock.

"Come in," he called. At least this time he took the time to look up from his work and give her a smile. "Hey, Mouse. You already done with your lesson? That was fast. I didn't even hear you."

"He didn't show up again." She searched his face, trying to discern his reaction.

A shrug. "You should call. That's not very professional of him."

She didn't respond.

"You going home then?"

"Yeah." She paused before shutting him back in his office. "How's your day going? How's budget stuff?"

"Oh, that's all done and taken care of."

"Did you get Nancy those receipts on time?"

"Yeah. Thanks for copying them. It'll be really nice to have that reimbursement check. I don't even know what I'm going to buy you for Christmas yet."

"I've already said you don't have to get me anything."

"But I want to. I hate to think of the way you grew up, knowing that I can't give you that kind of lifestyle."

"This is what I chose."

"I know, but you deserve better." He reached his hands out, and she automatically stepped forward to accept his hug. "I want to give you every good thing in the world. I love you, Mouse. I love you so much."

She would have given up music lessons for the rest of her life if she could have felt at that moment a fraction of the passion and romance they'd shared before their wedding. "I love you, too," she answered.

And my name's not Mouse, she wanted to add, but like always, her voice refused to cooperate.

CHAPTER 58

It had been a long afternoon, but Katrina was proud of all that she had accomplished. The laundry was folded and put away, and the only mess in the kitchen was one last batch of dishes drying on the counter that she'd clear first thing in the morning. As long as she could learn to keep up with these daily tasks and didn't fall behind, she could keep the house presentable so her husband wouldn't end up embarrassed anymore.

She'd been working on her attitude too. Just like she didn't want to let the chores pile up, she didn't want to let unconfessed sins set up a stronghold in her spirit again. She had to be constantly on guard against resentment. That would probably be her biggest struggle here in Orchard Grove, but if she conquered bitterness and learned to interact cheerfully with the members of her church, it'd be a huge spiritual victory.

She and Greg hadn't had any major blowups today. With only about half an hour left to go before they turned off the lights, they might finally make it through at least one day without some major marital catastrophe.

She brushed her teeth and got into bed. After the miscarriage, she'd grown somewhat lax in her daily Bible reading and was trying to get back into the habit. The problem was she didn't know where to start. Maybe something from Isaiah since that was the book Grandma Lucy had quoted so much during her Sunday prayer time.

Greg came in with a half smile and started changing into his flannel pajama pants. When they moved to Orchard Grove, he'd had the slightest roll of pudge around his midsection, which now had disappeared. Hopefully that was because she was a nutritious cook and not a terrible one.

"Have a good day?" He sat on the side of the bed. He'd been behind on his sermon prep this evening and had eaten dinner in his office, so this was one of the first times all day they found themselves together.

"Things went well." She thumbed through Isaiah, hoping for a passage that would catch her eye.

"You tired?" Greg asked, which was his usual way of finding out if she was feeling particularly romantic.

"A little."

He leaned forward and reached under the bed. "Well, don't go to sleep yet because I have an early Christmas present for you." He pulled out a gift bag with baby blue and yellow polka dots on a pastel background.

"I thought we weren't going to spend the money on gifts this year." Katrina set her Bible down.

"It wasn't that expensive. You want to open it now?"

"It's a little early."

He shrugged. "Go ahead."

Tentatively, she reached for the bag and pulled out a somewhat generic looking teddy bear. Not exactly what she had envisioned, but at least he was right about one thing. It wouldn't destroy their budget.

"It's really cute." She tried to infuse her voice with some facsimile of enthusiasm. "Thank you."

Greg took the stuffed animal out of her hands. "There's more." He turned it around and showed Katrina a zipper on its back. "Open it up."

The hole was so small once she got it unzipped she could only dig around with her fingers to find out what was in it. She pulled out a folded piece of glossy paper and opened it up. She knew that familiar image. The eight-week ultrasound the doctor had taken to confirm her pregnancy. "What's this for?"

He leaned over and gave the scarcely identifiable jellybean in the picture a soft caress with his finger. "I was reading this website the other day about grieving after miscarriage, and this was one of the ideas that came up. We never had a funeral or burial or anything, so I thought this might be a good way to remember our baby."

He reached into the small zipper pouch in the bear's back and pulled out another piece of paper. He didn't unfold it but held it up in his hand. "I wrote a letter. I felt silly when I started, but I think it was good for me. You can write something too if you want and keep it in here. But you don't have to."

Katrina was curious to find out what her husband might have written in his letter, but he tucked the paper back into the zipper pouch.

"That was a great idea. I love it." Katrina leaned in to give her husband a hug. "Thank you."

He frowned at her sympathetically. "You're not gonna start crying now, are you?"

"No, I wasn't planning on it."

He wrapped his arm around her. "Because you know I'm here for you."

She burrowed her face against his chest, slightly embarrassed that she wasn't as emotional as he apparently expected her to be. "Now I need to think of something to give you."

"You don't have to get me anything." He kissed the top of her head. "Everything I've always wanted is right here."

CHAPTER 59

Katrina tried to stay on top of her chores the following day, but she had a hard time focusing on any particular job. Instead of getting one task completely done, she'd spend five minutes shuffling things around on the kitchen counters, then make her way into the living room to see how much clutter there was to put away, and the whole time she'd been thinking about the dishes from breakfast and lunch that hadn't been washed yet. At some point in the early afternoon, she realized that for all her half efforts, she had absolutely no progress to show for it. She might as well stop trying until her brain was fully engaged in her work.

She opened up her case but didn't take Dmitry out. If Greg came home to a messy house, what would he think when he found her playing around on her violin instead of keeping up appearances and being the pastor's wife people expected her to be? She positioned herself by the window so she could see when he made his way home and tried a few of her vocal warmups. The effort was just as half-hearted as her cleaning attempts, and the entire time she sang she heard her mom's voice telling her how terrible she sounded.

Maybe Orchard Grove just wasn't the kind of place where she could conjure up her musical inspiration on demand. Unfortunately, Greg had already committed her to playing a solo at the Christmas Eve service. She really needed to start practicing. Her Christmas medley was all right, but she wanted to work more thoroughly through some of the transitions. Why had Greg volunteered her anyway?

Because she was Orchard Grove's pastor's wife.

No, that was the old way of thinking that would only lead to bitterness. God had given her a gift through her music, and she should be happy to use it for him and for his glory. If playing her violin at the Christmas Eve service could encourage others to worship the Lord more fully, she had no right to complain.

The doorbell rang. Greg was out for an afternoon of visitations, and Katrina wasn't expecting anybody. Whoever it was, why couldn't they have stopped by yesterday after she'd worked so hard to get the house clean?

The front door opened when she was still halfway down the hall.

"Katrina, dear?"

It was Mrs. Porter, who even after what happened last week still assumed it was safe to step into Katrina's house unannounced.

"Oh, there you are." Mrs. Porter exclaimed. "Where's your coat? We're already late."

"Late for what?"

"Didn't PG tell you? We've got all the kids singing carols today at the Winter Grove home for the elderly. PG's out with the car so I volunteered to drive over here and pick you up, but I was wrapping presents for the grandkids and lost track of time. Are you ready? Don't you need a coat? And what about that scarf I picked out for you?"

Katrina blinked, trying desperately to snap her brain and body into action. In all their brief interactions today, Greg hadn't said a single word about a home for the elderly. If he had volunteered her for one more musical commitment, she certainly would have remembered.

"I'll be there in a minute. Let me go grab my purse."

Mrs. Porter grabbed her arm. "I'm driving, so you won't need it. Come on. I already told you we're late."

***

Katrina had driven by the Winter Grove Assisted Living Home before but this was her first time inside. The few Christmas decorations in the main lobby weren't overstated but gave a certain homey feel to the large space. The building split off into three different wings, each with their own subtle color scheme.

"Now, don't be mad at us for being late, PG. It's not Katrina's fault. It was me, so don't be cross, and let's find out which wing they want us to start on. Is everyone here?" She did a quick count of the children, mumbling under her breath. "Well, my guess is that this will be it. If anybody comes in late, they'll just have to stop by the front desk and find out where we are." She turned to Katrina. "Now, you set up your violin and do whatever you need to do to get ready."

"My violin?"

"Yes, how else are we supposed to all sing together? I assumed PG had it since you didn't bring it with you."

"No," Katrina said. "It's at home."

Mrs. Porter let out a dramatic sigh. "Well, then, I don't know what to do. I don't suppose you thought to bring your guitar did you, PG?"

Greg shook his head. "No, but we can manage just fine *a cappella*, can't we?" Mrs. Porter started in on some diatribe about a dozen different kids singing in a dozen different keys, but Katrina interrupted before she could get to the monologue's climax.

"It's just a couple minutes to the house. I'll go get my violin and be right back." At least with her instrument, she wouldn't be expected to lead the music with her voice.

Mrs. Porter rolled her eyes at the clock, bemoaning how late they already were.

"It's not like the people here have anywhere else to be." Greg got his car keys and handed them to Katrina with a brief kiss on the cheek and mumbled, "Drive safely."

She was so thankful to free her ears from Mrs. Porter's whiny pitch that she hardly noticed how cold it was outside. She found Greg's car, and during the short drive back to the parsonage wondered how much of a scandal it would cause if she just stayed there at home without returning to Winter Grove at all.

It was an innocent daydream, similar to the way she would imagine talking back to her mom when she was a teen. Idle fantasies that she would never really act upon, but they gave her some sense of boldness, some illusion of control.

She pulled in front of the parsonage and hurried up the sidewalk, so distracted that she nearly collided into someone on the walkway.

"Kat. I've been looking all over for you. First here, then at the school."

Miles.

She blinked. Her one thought was she had to grab her violin and head back to Winter Grove before poor Mrs. Porter suffered a heart attack.

"Do you have a minute? I really want to talk to you."

She studied his face. Something about him, his expression, was different. Pained.

"I wish I could, but I just stopped by here to grab my violin for a thing we're doing with the church ..."

"Can I come back later? I'm so sorry for missing our lessons. But I really need to see you."

"I'm not sure how long this thing's going to take," Katrina told him. "I might be tied up for the rest of the day."

"Tomorrow then. We can meet here at the church at three like we had planned. Will that work for you?"

Katrina nodded. "That will work. Are you ok?"

He gave her a tired smile. "That's probably something we should talk about tomorrow." Katrina stared as he headed back to his truck and backed out of the church parking lot. After he drove off and disappeared from view, she remembered what she was doing here, ran in the house to get her violin, and tried to ignore the wild syncopated rhythm of her heart.

CHAPTER 60

When Katrina returned to the Winter Grove Assisted Living Home, Mrs. Porter was the only one from the church still in the lobby.

"Here you are," she huffed impatiently. "Well, come on. The kids were getting restless so I told them to go ahead and get started. I'll take you to where they're singing, and you can join them there."

Since the children could obviously perform Christmas carols without accompaniment, Katrina wondered why she'd bothered to race back home to get her violin at all, but at least she'd reconnected with Miles, even if only for a few seconds. What was it he so badly wanted to tell her, and why did she feel guilty about making plans to meet him at the church tomorrow without asking her husband first? It wasn't like Greg was her parent and had to give permission for every little thing she did. Besides that, Greg knew that they were planning on meeting each afternoon at the church anyway, so it wasn't even as if she'd made any new plans her husband didn't know about.

"I've always said that by the time I get up to the age of the residents here," Mrs. Porter was saying as they sped down one of the hallways, "I hope God spares me this unnecessary and prolonged suffering and just takes me right on home to glory." She gave a dramatic shiver. "I'm the last person on earth to go around believing in ghosts, but I've already told my children that if they even think of putting me in a home like this when I'm an old woman, I'll come back after I die and haunt them forever."

Katrina didn't think she was expected to respond, and soon she and Mrs. Porter arrived at a door with some handmade paper snowflakes taped beneath a sign labeled *Recreation*.

"Right in here," Mrs. Porter shoved Katrina through the door and into the rec room where the kids were in the middle of singing *We Three Kings*.

"Get your violin ready," Mrs. Porter nudged her in the ribs. "I hope you're already tuned up or whatever it is you musical types call it."

Greg was standing against the far wall and gave Katrina a small nod, just enough to acknowledge that he'd seen her enter. What was he thinking? Was he mad she was late? Did he suspect she'd seen Miles?

Katrina set her case on an empty chair and knelt to take out her violin.

The kids had already finished their song by the time Katrina was ready to play. They were on the second verse of *Silent Night* in a key that was halfway between D and D-sharp. There was technically no such thing as quarter position, but Katrina would have to do her best. At least for the next song, she would get to choose the starting note.

Katrina had been plunking out these Christmas carols from her earliest days on the violin, which unfortunately allowed her mind to wander. Why hadn't Miles been able to answer her question simply when she asked if something was wrong? It had been hard for her — no, impossible — to make any progress with her singing after he disappeared, so why did she experience so much foreboding and dread at the thought of meeting him tomorrow? And why was she disappointed that he'd chosen the church when she was the one who'd asked to stop meeting at the school?

She had to think about something else. She'd already been playing for nearly twenty minutes, but the audience gave no sign of wanting the performance to end.

When the residents' eyes weren't focused on her, Katrina studied their faces, trying to imagine what history was etched into each wrinkle. She thought about Mrs. Porter's disparaging remarks about nursing homes, but for what it was, Winter Grove was pleasant enough, with a staff that obviously took pains to maintain a cheerful atmosphere, at least from what Katrina could tell.

Most of the residents were what she would have expected at a place like this. Old men in wheelchairs. White-haired ladies smiling and tapping their feet to the beat. But there was one woman who seemed far too young for a place like this. There was more brown than gray in her hair, and her skin was free from wrinkles save for a few creases around her eyes that appeared like echoes of happiness on an otherwise tragic face. She stared into the distance with eyes half glazed, and she sat in her own corner somewhat removed from the rest of the group. Katrina couldn't pinpoint what it was that made her so intriguing, but — if for no other reason than her youthful features — she seemed so out of place.

She didn't belong in a home like this.

It wasn't until they'd fully exhausted the children's Christmas carol repertoire that the concert was declared finished. They would give two other repeat performances in the other wings of Winter Grove. By the time they finished, it would be past sunset.

Oh, well. If Katrina lived at an assisted living home, she'd want some music to listen to around Christmastime. Playing along on her violin was simple enough that maybe it would even pull her out of the little musical funk she'd been in for the past few days.

And besides, it beat sitting around a cluttered home worrying about whatever it was that Miles wanted to tell her tomorrow afternoon.

CHAPTER 61

"What's that you're playing?" Greg asked, peeking his head into the cry room.

It was far too cramped for Katrina to be practicing comfortably in here, but she needed to be alone. She couldn't articulate why she was so nervous about meeting Miles, but she could hardly hold onto her fingerboard without the sweat causing it to slip out of her hands.

She put down her bow. "Just some Bach."

Greg frowned. "Sounds complicated."

She shrugged. "Not really."

"Well, I'm heading out for a few hours."

"Where are you going?"

"Just to Winter Grove."

"The assisted living home? What for?"

"They asked me to lead a weekly Bible study. I told you about that last night. Remember?"

No, he hadn't told her. Or had she just forgotten?

"You're having your lesson soon?"

She answered with a nod, and he leaned over and pecked her on the cheek. "Well, have a good time with your scales and warmups and all that fun stuff." His smile was so carefree. So easy. How could he look that composed?

She did her best to smile back naturally but got the sense she failed. Fortunately, he was too preoccupied to notice. "I might swing by the store and run a few errands after that, so I'll see you in a while. Don't worry about holding dinner for me if I'm late."

One more peck on the cheek and he was gone.

Katrina stared at her bow. Her practice had been interrupted, and she was trying to figure out if it was worth the effort to move out of the cramped cry room and into the sanctuary when the door of the church swung open.

Her heart was racing. She wiped her sweaty palms on her pants. Why had she worn her jeans and this plain sweater? What Mrs. Porter told her back at the Safe Anchorage Gift Shop was true. Winter was no time for pastels.

Oh, well. Too late now.

She stepped out of the cry room.

Miles stared at her, his eyes shining, his face flushed. "I'm so glad you're here. I really need to talk to you."

She glanced at the door her husband had so recently stepped out of and found herself longing for the safety and protection of the claustrophobic closet she'd just left.

He took her by the wrist and led her into the sanctuary. "I should have warned you from the beginning," he said. "I sometimes get this idea in my head that I'm actually decent at composing, and when I'm working on something I sort of tune out the whole world for a few days. I'm really sorry about that. I know I missed our lessons, and I feel terrible. But I'm really hoping this will make it up to you."

He sat her down in the front pew, reached into his pocket, and pulled out his phone.

"Here."

"What am I looking at?" She stared at the screen.

"It's the piece I wrote. I guess you could say I was inspired the last time we sang together. I wanted to come up with something for Christmas. Something to showcase your talent." He reached across her and scrolled ahead on his screen. "See, I even wrote a part for your violin."

She blinked as the notes on the screen transformed themselves into music in her mind.

"So this is what you've been working on?" Was that all she could come up with to say?

"Yeah. It's, well, I sort of did it for you. I mean for us. I thought that maybe if you were interested, you could come over. I have a little recording studio. It's nothing fancy, so don't get your expectations too high or anything. It's just this little amateur thing, but with your violin and the way we sound when we sing together ... I just thought maybe we could make ourselves a recording."

"Like formally?" When had she started talking like a valley girl? And why was she still so focused on the fact that she'd worn pastel in the middle of December?

"Sure. I mean, I've laid out a few songs before. Nothing's really taken off, but I've got a small following on a few of the indie platforms. I just ... We sang together the other day, and I couldn't get your voice out of my head, and then I thought with your violin ..." He finally took in an inhale. "Tell me what you're thinking. You look a little stunned."

What was she supposed to say? Accompanying a musician on her violin was one thing, but laying out a track on vocals ...

"You don't have to say yes right away, but would you at least run through it with me a time or two? I've hardly slept since we were together last, and I know I'll never be able to rest or relax until I hear it. Because sometimes these things sound a lot different in your head than they do in real life, and I'm not too full of myself to admit that maybe it's just junk, but I really think I've got something here."

She hadn't ever heard him so animated, seen his face

shine with such excitement. She held his phone, still listening to the way the violin part played out in her mind. Miles was clearly an intuitive composer. The refrains accentuated all of the strongest aspects of Katrina's playing, as if he'd written the piece entirely for her.

Which, now that she thought about it, he had.

He stared at her with an earnestness that made him appear a decade or more younger. Like a teenager asking his long-time crush to dance with him. "Will you try it out with me? Just this once?"

She was drawn to his eyes. Remembered vividly the musical connection they'd made the last time they were together at the school. Recalled how anxious she'd felt during the past few days when she hadn't been able to meet with him.

She glanced back down at his screen, focusing on the vocal parts. Hers would be mostly harmony. It wasn't anything too tricky or demanding.

What could it hurt?

"Sure." She handed him his phone.

His entire face beamed at her, joy unbridled like a child's on Christmas morning.

She couldn't help but smile back. Genuinely this time. She fidgeted with her ring, her eyes still interlocked with his. "Let's try it and see how it goes."

CHAPTER 62

She set down her bow, the music from her violin and his voice still ringing in the sanctuary.

He stared at her. Intently. So focused. As if his gaze on her face was what kept the breath flowing in and out of her lungs.

She didn't want to speak. Didn't want to break the spell their music had cast over the room, the entire town of Orchard Grove.

The only noise she could hear over her pulse in her ears was the echo of the refrain he'd just sung.

He took a step closer to her. She could feel his energy, his strength. How could someone with this level of musical genius live in a desert like this? How did he keep his inspiration from drying up like the Orchard Grove riverbed?

How had he composed a piece that would stretch and challenge her voice while still accentuating her strengths?

And the violin solo. She'd never had a piece written specifically for her, never even dreamed of a composer granting her that honor.

Singing with Miles that last time at the school had left her breathless, panting, confused.

Now, she felt more at peace than she had in her entire adult life.

This was what she had been meant to do. To create beautiful music, music like this. How had she lost sight of that for so many months? How had she survived in Orchard Grove before she met Miles and experienced the beauty of his creative expression?

He'd done far more for her than write a simple song. He was the key that had unlocked her voice, held captive her entire life. His encouragement had shattered all the lies her mother told her about how she could never sing, could scarcely even hold a tune. He'd found her voice and handed it to her in a golden box, and as if that weren't enough, he'd helped her heal from the musical dry spell that had kept her separated from her beloved violin, her Dmitry.

How could she ever repay him?

"So you'll come to my studio and record with me?" he asked. So hopeful. Endearing.

The teenage boy at his first boy-girl party, asking Katrina to dance, terrified she would turn him down.

She couldn't do that to him.

She wouldn't.

The truth was she wanted to record with him. Wanted to push her musical abilities to new limits, discover what it meant to be freed from these constraints that had kept her silenced for so long.

"Sure," she answered and watched his face melt into joy. The feeling was contagious, and she had to stifle a giggle. "I'd love to."

He swiped his screen to get it to the beginning of the piece. "All right. Well, then, let's get to work. We have a lot to practice."

CHAPTER 63

Katrina hurried home a few minutes before six, terrified she'd find Greg at the parsonage waiting, wondering what she and her teacher had been doing for the past three hours.

Thankfully, he was late, just like he'd warned her. She threw a meatloaf together, prayed it would stick, and while it cooked in the oven she sprinted around the house, tidying up with the speed and energy of Rimsky-Korsakov's iconic *Bumblebee*.

Greg still wasn't home by the time dinner was ready, which was probably a blessing. The meatloaf was charred, and the veggies were limp and bland. He wasn't missing out on much. She ate alone in silence, her appetite fueled by her mad dash around the house as well as her excited nerves about recording with Miles in his studio.

She'd have to talk to her husband, make sure he felt it would be appropriate, but she couldn't imagine him denying her request. Besides, with as distracted as he'd been, she could probably ask him for permission to visit the White

House, and he'd mumble his assent without even thinking through her question.

At least that's what she was hoping for.

She'd never seen anyone as eager and enthusiastic as Miles had been. As soon as she told him she'd try to lay down his new song with him, he rambled on so long about the different plans he had for their recording. She believed him when he said he hadn't thought about anything else in days. He already had ideas for a music video, knew a guy who could handle the editing, and was even talking about ways they could get their song onto some of the paying platforms.

And he wanted it all done in time for Christmas.

His enthusiasm was catching, and it wasn't until he left for home to make some final arrangements for their recording session that she felt the first pang or two of trepidation. What if Greg thought it was a waste of time?

What would the members of the church say? Would they find it odd that their pastor's wife was recording a secular song with another man? At least it wasn't a typical love song. Miles' lyrics had far more depth than a cheesy chorus and repeated lines about love and kisses and beauty. But there were undertones, nuances in the lyrics that certainly spoke of longing and intimacy if you listened carefully.

While she ate her mediocre dinner alone, she tried to

think of the best way to present it to her husband. *He could use a little help on vocals and asked if I'd be willing to try it out. He really wants to record it but needs a female singer. It's a small way I can repay him for giving me all those voice lessons for free.*

Recalling how budget-conscious Greg had become of late, she figured she would make this last point her sticking one.

When she heard the front door open, she jumped to her feet. "Hi, honey," she called as cheerfully as she could. "I made some meatloaf. It's not even cold yet."

Greg was in the entrance, kicking off his boots and tossing his coat onto the hanger.

She strained her eyes, searching for signs of tension or anger that might warn her about her husband's mood.

"How'd your afternoon go?" She hated the way she sounded so small. Maybe one day she'd ask Miles if he could do for her speaking voice what he'd done for her singing. The key to that sort of confidence must be there somewhere. She could find it if she tried hard enough.

Or if she had the right teacher to show her where to look.

Greg still hadn't said anything. Was that a bad sign? "You all right?"

He nodded. "Just tired." He pecked her on the cheek. "Mmm. Smells good. What'd you make?"

"Just some meatloaf and veggies. I can fix some mashed potatoes or something too if you want."

He shook his head. "I ate already."

"You did?"

"Yeah, I ran into Nancy Higgins at Walmart, and she had a few questions about the budget, so we grabbed burgers at the food court."

If Greg's mind had been on the budget all afternoon, she definitely didn't want to bring up anything that might upset him even more. "Is everything ok? With the budget, I mean?"

"Oh, yeah. There were just a few things I marked down in different spots than she's used to, so we went over that and it was fine."

"Ok." Well, if her husband could go out for dinner with a female member of the church without it turning into a big, major deal, there was no reason she shouldn't go to the recording studio with Miles. She smiled at her husband, realizing how thankful she was to have him home, how quiet the parsonage had been since she got back from practicing at the church.

"Tell me about your day," he said then glanced around the living room. "The house looks really good, by the way. I can tell you've worked hard. Is that what you've been up to all afternoon?"

"Mostly." She headed back toward the dining room, but he took her hand and pulled her toward him. After giving her a much more proper kiss, he pulled back but still held her hand. "Well, that was a nice hello."

She smiled back and giggled when he wouldn't let her go back to the table to finish her food. So her husband had met with the church treasurer and come home in a good mood.

Who said there were no such things as Christmas miracles?

CHAPTER 64

"So what's he want to do with this song?" Greg asked.

Katrina lay on her back in bed, staring up at the ceiling. "Just to record it. He's got a little studio set up. Nothing fancy, but it's got the right kind of equipment and stuff. I just wanted to make sure it was all right with you."

He shrugged. "Why wouldn't it be?"

Katrina didn't want to list the reasons out for him, so she twisted her wedding ring and answered, "Oh, you know how weird some people get around here. I mean, it's not a bad song or anything, but it's not Christian, and well, I just wanted to get your opinion before I agreed to anything officially."

He leaned over and kissed her nose. "Sure. It sounds fun. I think you should go for it."

"Really?"

"Yeah, if you want to. I'm glad to see you getting back into your music. It's been a quiet couple of months around here."

"Yeah, it has."

He reached out and twirled some of her hair around his

finger. "I'm really glad you and Miles met. He seems like a neat guy. Does he have any family around here? Other than the Porters, I mean."

Katrina stretched her mind back over their interactions. They'd shared so much musically that she was surprised she didn't know the answer to this very basic question. "Actually, I'm not sure."

Greg shrugged again. "Well, I have to wake up pretty early to get working on my sermon, so I'm going to say goodnight."

Katrina stared up at the cottage-cheese constellations on their ceiling, her fingers playing into her palm as if on an imaginary violin.

"Goodnight," she answered back, while her ears echoed with Miles' song.

CHAPTER 65

Her first knock was so timid she had to repeat herself twice before Miles opened his front door.

"Oh, good," he breathed. "I kept worrying that you were going to change your mind and back out."

She glanced at the clock behind his shoulder. "Sorry, the roads were a little icy, and I got a later start than I hoped."

"Don't worry about it." He stood aside to let her in. "I'm just glad you're here. I couldn't sleep last night, I was so excited. I can't begin to tell you how thankful I am that you've agreed to do this. I haven't been this inspired with my music for years. In fact, I was considering leaving Orchard Grove. It just seemed like all my creativity died the day I moved here."

She nodded. "I understand."

"Can I take your coat?"

She'd be embarrassed if he knew how long she'd deliberated over what she should wear. If they made a music video like he hoped, it wouldn't be of the two of them, but even though she knew she wouldn't be in front of the camera, she'd tried on half a dozen different outfits or more. What had gotten into her? She'd been performing nearly her entire life. Why should she feel so nervous now?

"I'm so glad you came," he repeated and led her down the hall. "Come this way. I'll show you my studio. Or do you want some tea first?"

She'd been so nervous all morning she'd hardly drunk anything, but she knew she was too anxious to carry any sort of conversation over tea. "I'm all right."

She followed him to his studio, a walk-in closet he'd converted to serve his purposes. He had the covers of several jazz albums on the wall, a large desktop computer, and a variety of microphones and other equipment strewn about.

"Welcome to my lair." He smiled, but even though he was obviously pleased to have her as his guest, there was no way for her to feel comfortable. At least not until they started playing together, and then hopefully the beauty of their harmony would drown out all her concerns.

"Are you really sure I should go?" she'd asked her husband that morning.

"If you want to," he answered with a shrug.

His response had disappointed her, even though she couldn't articulate why. Had she been hoping Greg would give her an excuse to bow out? Had her stage fright stolen away her new confidence?

Or were there other reasons why she still felt uncertain about being here?

It was her mother, probably, all those years her mom spent complaining about men like Miles, living off his teacher's salary and engrossed in artistic endeavors that would never make him rich or famous or powerful or important or give him any of the other status symbols her mother so highly coveted.

The more Katrina thought about it, the more she realized how similar he was to her husband. One pursued ministry, the other music, but both were passionate, devoted to their work, sometimes to a fault. Neither would earn his millions or leave a lasting mark outside of his small sphere of influence.

Two men with such different pursuits, but on the other hand so similar.

She remembered how strange it had felt last night when Greg asked about Miles' family and she'd realized she knew so little about his personal life. Had he ever been married? Ever loved someone else with the same passion he devoted to his music?

Then again, what business was it of hers anyway? She was here to help him record a song, something she could easily do without knowing his entire life history.

"Should I take out my violin?" she asked.

He shook his head. "Not yet. I figure we'll be lucky if we get the vocals laid out by lunchtime. We can worry about instrumentals after that."

Katrina realized she had no idea how long recording a song was supposed to take, but she tried to hide her surprise.

"Are you warmed up?" he asked.

She rubbed her hands together. "I'm fine. I had the heat up on high in the car, and I'm still pretty toasty."

His smile was soft and gentle. "I meant your voice."

She lowered her gaze. "Oh. No, I haven't done much yet today." Maybe she should have spent more effort preparing her voice instead of spending all that time trying to find something to wear that wasn't pastel.

He turned around in his swivel chair and pushed a button on his keyboard. "All right, then. First things first. Let's get you ready to sing."

CHAPTER 66

You still there? How's it going?

Katrina stared at her husband's text.

"Everything all right?" Miles asked.

She was quick to nod. "Yeah, I … Um, mind if I step out for a few minutes?"

He warmed her with the genuineness of his smile. "Take as long as you need. It's probably time we rested your voice anyway. Make yourself comfortable."

She took her phone and tried to be as unobtrusive as she could while exiting his small studio. She had to pass through his bedroom on the way to the living room, and she glanced around at the sparse furniture, the few piles of magazines, clothes, and books that made the room look comfortably lived in but not cluttered.

She called her husband and held the phone to her ear, wondering if Miles would mind if she got herself a cup of water.

"Hey, Mouse." Greg's voice startled her. She hadn't

expected him to answer on the first ring. "How's my little recording diva?"

For the past three hours in Miles' studio, she hadn't realized how tight and strained her voice was, but every muscle in her throat now screamed with exhaustion.

"All right."

"What'd you say? You're talking really quiet."

She tried to wet her vocal cords with a swallow. "It's going all right."

"Yeah, you almost done? I thought maybe we could go out for lunch or something."

"That's really sweet, but I think this is going to take us a while. We just got past the first verse and that's all so far."

"Really? How long does he expect you to stay there?"

She glanced down the hall to see if Miles had come out of his studio. "It'll probably still be a while."

"What are you going to do about food? It's already past lunchtime."

"I think he said something about grabbing a bite here soon before we get back to work." Suddenly aware of how sweaty her hands had grown, she wiped her palm against her red sweater.

"He's just expecting you to do this all day, and he's not paying you anything?"

"We haven't talked about that, really." She kept her voice low, not just because it hurt to speak but because she didn't feel now was the appropriate time for this conversation. Not while she was standing in the middle of Miles' kitchen looking for the cupboard where he kept his cups.

"You need to get that sort of information up front, you know. If he's going to be making any money off this song you're helping with, you're entitled to your fair share."

She should be relieved that he was fixating on the finances and not on the fact that she'd been alone in a closet off some single guy's bedroom all morning with no intentions of coming home soon. "We'll talk about it, and I'll let you know, ok?"

"Well, make sure to stand up for yourself. I know that's not always the easiest thing for you to do, but if you don't, nobody else is gonna do it for you."

"Yeah, ok." She hoped he'd end the call soon. She just needed five minutes. Five minutes without having to use her voice. Five minutes to herself, to collect her thoughts, process the past few hours. She'd had no idea when she agreed to record with Miles how long of an ordeal it was. She knew big-name artists could work this hard, but she figured a song that would only get a few hundred hits on YouTube if it was lucky would be far simpler.

Showed how much she knew.

"Call me when you're done, all right? And I need you home by three because I have to take the car to go with the Higginses to deliver some of those meals they've been collecting. I guess that's it." He paused for a moment. "Are you having fun, Mouse?"

She nodded even though he obviously couldn't see the gesture. "Yeah. It's been good."

"All right. Just come home by three. Don't be late."

She ended the call and pulled down one of Miles' Hard Rock Café mugs.

"Everything all right?" His voice behind her made her jump in surprise. "Sorry. I thought you heard me coming out."

She paused just a moment before turning around. Just a moment where she didn't have to use her voice or think about music or recording or her husband or when she had to have the car back to the parsonage. Just long enough to catch her breath, and then she turned to face him.

"You look tired." His stare was so intense, his expression so frank. It was that intuition of his that made him such a good teacher but also made her feel uncomfortable when they weren't making music together.

"I am." She did her best to smile, hoping he wouldn't be upset that she'd rummaged through his kitchen cabinets.

"Well, you're doing great, but I know it's been a long morning."

She didn't mention it was already afternoon.

He opened the fridge. "I got us a special laying-out lunch ready." He pulled out some grapes, carrot slices, avocado, and smoked salmon, explaining how each of the ingredients were supposed to soothe her throat or strengthen her voice. "And of course ..." He held up an empty pot. "Plenty of tea."

After he refused to let her help the third time she offered, she sat down in the dining room and watched him set everything up. While he was chopping a lemon for their tea, he asked, "So, what's it like being a pastor's wife?"

Thankful his back was to her, she tried to figure out what she wanted to say.

"I imagine Orchard Grove isn't the easiest of churches," he went on. "Lots of people to try to keep happy, right?"

"Something like that."

He turned to face her. "Well, for what it's worth, I'm sure it's a stressful position from time to time, and I really admire you for sticking with it. My aunt raves about you, by the way, talks about how everyone there just adores you."

Katrina couldn't pinpoint which was more surprising, that Mrs. Porter could be said to rave about anybody or that she'd had something kind to say about Katrina herself. Or maybe Miles was just being nice. Maybe he knew she was tired and frustrated after a long morning of recording and could use a confidence boost.

"Does your husband like what he does?" He glanced at her out of the corner of his eye before adding the lemon slices to their tea.

Katrina bit her lip. "It has its ups and downs, but we're really glad to be here." Sadly, this partial truth was far more honest than anything she'd ever said to anyone at church. At least she'd admitted that the position wasn't perfect.

Miles brought their plates over, reached out for their mugs, and sat down beside her. His table was so small their knees nearly touched. He didn't seem to notice but spread some peanut butter on his banana. "Well, for what it's worth, that church has had a whole string of lousy pastors. So as long as your husband doesn't follow in any of their footsteps, I think you're both going to do just fine."

Katrina had already heard the rundown of several of her husband's predecessors and their myriad faults. She wanted to find a way to change the subject but didn't know where to begin. When they weren't talking about the music they both loved, what was there between them?

"So tell me about growing up in California," he said. "That's where you're from, right?"

Katrina took a sip of tea. It scalded her tongue, but the honey ran warm down her throat, relieving her strained vocal cords. "What do you want to know?"

"Anything. Tell me about your mom."

She let out a small chuckle. "How much time do you have?"

CHAPTER 67

An hour later, with Miles still refusing to let her help clean up, Katrina sat at his small table while he put the leftovers away. She couldn't believe how long she'd talked. It was a good thing they'd agreed to work on instrumentals next. Her voice had been strained even before they spent all of lunch break discussing her childhood, her music, and most of all her mother.

"She kind of sounds like a freak." It didn't take long for Miles to reach his conclusion.

When the table was clear, he gave her the smile that had grown so familiar. "You ready for round two?"

She nodded.

"Ok, and you just tell me when you're tired and ready to call it a day, all right?"

"I will." She had never been so ready to pull out her violin. Ready to give her vocal cords a break and let her instrument take over.

Let Dmitry sing.

"I can't wait to hear how this turns out." Miles grinned and held the door to his studio closet open for her. The room was so small she'd have to remind herself not to sway too much or she really might poke his eye out with her bow.

She went straight to her case, but Miles stopped her. "Wait a minute."

She turned to him. She hoped her breath didn't stink from all that salmon.

He stared down at her, and she did her best to catch her breath.

"I just want to tell you how thankful I am that you're doing this for me. I said it before, but I'm not sure you understand. Before we met, I'd gone four years without composing anything. Four whole years."

She tried imagining that long without Dmitry but couldn't. The few months she'd taken off from her violin had been empty enough.

"You're a gift from heaven," he confessed, even though he'd never spoken about God in any personal way before. "My muse." He stopped. "Am I making you uncomfortable by saying that?"

How was she supposed to respond when she couldn't breathe? What was she supposed to say if all the air had fled the room?

"I don't want to do anything that would make you uncomfortable." He spoke the words softly, with a question tacked on to the end. An invitation.

One she found herself responding to implicitly the longer she stayed silent.

Something. She had to do something. Say something. But this same man who'd so recently helped her discover her voice had now stolen it away.

"I think we're really similar." His words were lulling. Hypnotic. "Two creative beings trapped in such a drab, colorless town with no art or beauty except what we create together." He paused.

She was ready to pull out her violin, but she'd forgotten how to say so.

Or maybe she'd never known how to begin with.

"I have a story for you."

She let out her breath as he eased himself into his swivel chair. Whatever it was that had just happened, whatever trance his words had pulled her into, the moment had passed. The air returned — normal, breathable, pure air.

She'd never take her own breath for granted again.

"Last year, I had two students," he began, "both of them great musicians." He picked at some lint on his pants leg. "Played the clarinet and flute, both first chair, both

315

extremely talented. Best kids I've worked with in years."

She nodded, uncertain why he was telling her some tale from his classroom but infinitely thankful he'd stopped talking about the way she'd become his muse and had inspired his music. Silly of her to get worked up over something that small. Silly to think that a harmless compliment was anything to leave her feeling so scared and weak and vulnerable.

"So when it came time for state Solo and Ensemble," he went on, "I paired them up. Thought they'd make the perfect match. I mean, these are really committed kids we're talking about here. Even had them coming over to the classroom two, three afternoons a week for extra practice. But you know what? Even though they were my two best students and on the surface it had made all the sense in the world to put them together, it turned out they just didn't cut it as a duet."

He glanced up from his pants and stole her breath once more with the intensity of his stare.

"Sometimes you get matched up with the wrong partner."

Blink.

She wanted to ask what happened next. Wanted to tell him that was an interesting story and then move on to start unpacking her instrument, but he held her gaze steady.

Blink.

She reached to fidget with her wedding ring but clenched her fists instead.

"Sometimes you get matched up with the wrong partner. But if you're lucky, you'll find the opportunity to make adjustments as necessary."

Blink.

The same gaze that held her captive also contained a thousand questions. A thousand ways for her to respond.

Blink.

"Do you get what I'm saying?"

She nodded, not because she wanted to agree with him but because she hoped that some response, any response, might free her from his stare.

He stood up again, his chest just inches away from hers. She stared at his shoulder, trying hard to resist the eyes that pulled her gaze toward his.

"Since that day we sang together, I've thanked God for bringing you here to Orchard Grove. You pulled me out of a four-year-long rut. I can never repay you for that."

Her head was spinning, her entire field of vision swallowed up by his nearness. She tried to blink her sight into focus, but it was impossible.

"Am I making you uncomfortable?" He'd asked her that

once before. Why hadn't she said something then? The longer she waited ...

But then again, why shouldn't an adult be able to compliment another adult without it turning into some big, weird, awkward thing? Why couldn't he tell her how thankful he was for the way she'd inspired him musically without her breath automatically escaping and her strength seeping out of every muscle in her body?

Why couldn't he express his gratitude?

Why shouldn't he?

It was silly for her to be so worked up. Silly and juvenile and vain, too. How full of herself did she have to be if she could honestly misconstrue one kind word to mean that he wanted to ...

His hands found her hips and pulled her close. His breath brushed softly against her temple when he whispered, "Tell me if you want me to stop." The corner of his mouth found the spot right above her eyebrow.

Her heart leaped so high into her throat she wouldn't have been able to speak even if she knew what to say. She doubted there was even a centimeter of space left separating her body from his, and yet he pulled her closer.

"I think we make a perfect duet," he mumbled into her skin.

Her heart was pounding so hard and he had pulled her so

tightly against his chest that she was certain each thud reverberated against him with the intensity of a mallet against a tympani drum.

She'd hesitated too long. If she were going to say something, it was too late now. Her silence had already made her complicit. She felt like the virgin at the end of *Rite of Spring*, about to meet her death in a gruesome pagan sacrifice.

A virgin who perhaps could have fought harder for her freedom than she did.

And all she could do was watch as if she were nothing more than a player in an orchestra, with the score set and predetermined long before she picked up her instrument.

There was nothing she could do.

Her body trembled against his, and he pulled her in closer, his lips now against her ear. "I won't do anything you don't want me to do."

That was it. Her one last chance of escape. If she didn't cling to it now, there would be no other way out.

She'd spent her entire lifetime being told that she was quiet. That she was demure. That she was nothing but a little voiceless mouse.

Except that wasn't who she was.

Not anymore.

"Stop." Her body still trembled, but her voice was firm. She pulled herself away and repeated that freeing word. "Stop."

He let out a breath large enough to fill the entire room.

So that's where all the air had gone. "Kat, I'm sorry ..."

She grabbed her violin case, and he stepped aside.

"I didn't want ... I didn't mean ..." He threw up his hands in a hopeless gesture.

"I need to go." She was prepared for a fight, but he let her walk by and didn't follow her out of his studio.

"I hope one day you'll forgive me," he called after her in a voice that had now lost its confidence as well as its allure.

CHAPTER 68

Home. She had to get herself home, yet it remained the last place she wanted to be right now. The last place, that is, besides Miles' small studio.

Or maybe she was deceiving herself. Wasn't there part of her that had wanted to stay? Did that make her a terrible person? Was wondering what might have happened just as bad as if it really had happened? It was too confusing to sort through everything right now. All she knew was that she needed to be home, but she was terrified of facing her husband.

None of the marriage books she'd read in the past year had prepared her for anything like this. There was no chapter called "what to do when your voice teacher tries to seduce you, and you almost comply."

She had to clear her mind. Figure out what she was supposed to tell Greg. If she was supposed to say anything. Would telling him just make it worse?

She couldn't think about that right now. She wouldn't. She drove aimlessly around Orchard Grove, doing everything she could to stop imagining what had almost happened — and what had already happened — in Miles' recording studio.

Was it her fault? She did say no, right? She did the right thing. But first there had been that moment of paralysis, that moment of hesitation.

If Miles hadn't told her for the final time that he would stop if she told him to, what would have happened then?

Would she always think about today with this mix of both overwhelming shame as well as an unwanted dose of curiosity? Would there always be a part of her that wondered … No. She couldn't think like that. Didn't Jesus himself teach that mental infidelity was just as sinful as the act itself?

How far had she let things go? And how much was she to blame? Should she be proud for leaving when she did or guilty for letting things progress to that point in the first place?

Her body was trembling, a clash of emotions and fears and adrenaline and shameful desires she tried not to acknowledge. She flicked on the windshield wipers several times before realizing that it was her tears distorting her vision, not the melted snow.

Clear her brain, seize control of her emotions, and then go home. After that, she could decide what she would or wouldn't tell Greg.

She needed to talk to somebody. Somewhere on the planet

Katrina was convinced was another woman who'd gone through something similar, but how would she find that person without exposing her shame to this town full of gossips?

No, it had to be someone on the outside. Someone who wouldn't turn around and call the prayer chain or talk about her in the ladies' bathroom while Katrina sat hunched and hidden in a stall.

Where could she find someone like that?

A picture flashed in her mind. Shock white hair, rounded spectacles always slipping off her nose, blouses with oversized collars that had been considered old-fashioned when Katrina's mom was a child.

Grandma Lucy.

A few minutes later, she parked her car in front of the Safe Anchorage Gift Shop and tried to work up the nerve to go in. It sounded like such a good idea on the drive over, but now that she was here, she was crippled with second guesses.

She hardly knew the eccentric old woman. How in the world do you start a conversation like the one she needed? *Hey, Grandma Lucy, I know how much you like to talk to God, so I've come here with a prayer request. See, there's this guy I almost had an affair with.*

No. It was stupid for her to come here. There was no use going on and on and talking about what might have happened or what almost happened in Miles' studio. She needed to get to her own house and do what she could to move on. She started up the car again when someone knocked on the passenger window.

Nancy Higgins. Great. Now that the church treasurer had spotted her here, Katrina would have to go into the store and make some pretense of looking around.

Nancy knocked again, and Katrina did her best to compose herself as she reached over to unlock the door.

"Brrr, it's cold out there. Mind if I sit down?" Nancy pulled the door shut after her. "I just stopped by for a few candles to add to the Christmas boxes we're passing out this afternoon. How are you, dear? Are you shopping for presents? My word, child. Your eyes are positively blotchy. Have you been crying?" She lowered her voice. "Is it about the baby?"

Katrina bit her lip until she was sure she was close to drawing blood and shook her head. Still gripping the steering wheel, she prayed Nancy would go away and leave her in peace.

"Well," Nancy sighed. "I don't pretend to know what's going on, and it's not my place to try to guess, but you sound like you could use a friend, and I hate to say it, but sometimes true and open friendships can be hard to come by in a town like this. So if you ever want to talk ..." Her voice trailed off.

What kind of pastor's wife was she? Poor Nancy probably thought Katrina was crying because Greg had run out of ice melt and one of the elders had yelled at him, or she was homesick and wished she could fly home to be with her mom this Christmas.

What kind of pastor's wife almost does what Katrina almost did? What kind of pastor's wife would ever even put herself in that sort of situation?

For a fleeting second, she thought about telling Nancy everything, unburdening her soul, painful and awkward and ugly as it would be. At least then she wouldn't be forced to carry this shame around with her like a burning secret. Nancy wasn't as terrible of a gossip as Mrs. Porter, and beneath her somewhat brusque exterior Katrina knew was a compassionate heart. A maternal heart. Someone who could guide Katrina and tell her what she was supposed to do next.

But she couldn't talk about it. She was the first lady of Orchard Grove Bible Church, and if anyone in her husband's congregation found out what she had nearly done …

Katrina wiped her eyes. "I'm sorry, it's just been a really busy week, and I think all the holiday stress has got me a little worn down."

Nancy nodded. "I understand completely. By the way, did your doctor tell you to take extra iron supplements after the miscarriage? You've got to be real careful about anemia, because it can sap your energy like that." She snapped her fingers in the air.

Katrina forced a wavering smile. "I'll be ok. Just holiday stress."

"That's perfectly normal."

Katrina nearly laughed. If Nancy could only guess the real reason for these tears.

"Thank you for checking on me," she finally said. "I think I'll just go home and rest for a little bit."

Nancy nodded sagely. "That's a good idea. And remember, you can always call me if there's anything you want to get off your chest. I'm not going to pretend like Orchard Grove Bible's an easy church to work for, and you're so young, and you and Pastor Greg have only been married for a few months, but for what it's worth, I think you're both doing a fantastic job."

After everything she'd just gone through, it was silly for Katrina to cling so tightly to Nancy's words, but she would take any small comfort she could get. "Thank you." She hoped Nancy could hear the sincerity in her voice. After few more of the expected pleasant exchanges, Nancy left and headed up toward the gift shop. Katrina put the car into reverse, took a deep breath, and mentally prepared herself for the trip home.

CHAPTER 69

"Hi there, Mouse."

Katrina was thankful to find her husband busy putting on his boots. He didn't try to kiss her when she walked in the door. How long would it take before he could touch her again without sending a flood of unwanted memories coursing through her?

"You're back just in time. I really want you to tell me all about your recording session, but I've got to run and make these deliveries. You have the keys?"

Katrina nodded and tried to look busy digging through her purse so she didn't have to meet his eyes.

"Hate to have to run, but I shouldn't be more than an hour or so. See you soon, and then you can tell me all about your first step on the road to stardom." He flashed a smile, reminding Katrina how handsome he looked when he was genuinely happy.

You're both doing a fantastic job, Nancy had said. And didn't Miles say Mrs. Porter had mentioned something similar?

No, Miles was no longer welcome in her thoughts. She didn't even want to think his name. But how could she forget?

"You ok?" Greg asked, cocking his head to the side and studying her.

"Yeah, just tired. I think I'll take a soak in the tub. I'm a little chilled."

"Well, just don't waste too much water, all right? I'll be back soon. Love you."

"I love you too," she answered, thankful that her voice didn't waver as he walked out the door.

CHAPTER 70

Katrina stepped out of the tub, no more certain about what she was supposed to do now than she had been when she first started bathing. For all the times her husband stayed out late on all his errands for the church, she hoped this would be one of them. She wasn't ready for him to come home. Not yet.

But being here by herself was nearly as bad. Once Greg got home, she'd have to decide if she was going to pretend that everything was just fine or if she was going to tell him about what happened. Talking about her afternoon would be painful and awkward and exhausting. But it was just as painful and awkward and exhausting to be abandoned to the mercy of her own memories and guilt. She was so ashamed, she didn't even want to pray, didn't want to face the reality of God's disappointment in her. Her mom was right. Katrina just wasn't the kind of person who could pull off the role of pastor's wife. Never had that been made clearer than this afternoon.

Shameful memories burned her core. She had gone into the

bath with a chill and came out sweaty and even more uncomfortable.

The house needed a little bit of work, but even though she carried herself from one cluttered room to another, she couldn't force her limbs to pick anything up. Today more than any other, the clock was her enemy, counting down the seconds until her husband returned. What should she do? She and Greg had gone into the marriage assuming that there would never be secrets between them, but who plans to almost have an affair only six months after the wedding? It was unforgivable. That's what it was. And if she wanted to keep up any semblance of peace with her husband, he could never know about this afternoon in Miles' studio.

But on the other hand, she had done the right thing by walking away. By keeping the truth from her husband, wasn't she admitting her own culpability? If she truly had nothing to hide, she would tell her husband everything and be done with it.

But was that the loving thing to do? Wouldn't it make him even more upset? And with all the stress he'd been under from work, wouldn't it be selfish of her to dump this on him on top of everything else he had to deal with?

She hated the thought of keeping a secret like this, but what choice did she have?

She'd been so distraught when she first came home she didn't realize until after her bath that she'd left her violin case in the cold entryway. She hoped that Dmitry would be more forgiving toward her than she was toward herself right now. From the front window, she saw a light on at the church. Great.

She threw on her boots and rushed outside, pausing for a moment on the porch. All traffic in and around Orchard Grove passed by this way. What if Miles drove by? What if he saw her? It was stupid to think that in a town this small she could spend the rest of her life here simply avoiding him, pretending he didn't exist, acting as if she'd never felt his body pressed against her, never sensed the warmth of his breath on her neck.

She ran to the church, nearly tripping on the icy walkway. She turned off the light in her husband's office then hurried home and locked herself back inside the parsonage. This was stupid. She couldn't hide forever in this little tiny house. Oh, well. She didn't have the energy to think about that right now. Greg would be home any minute, and she wasn't ready to face him. She took Dmitry into the bedroom and was about to tuck her case beneath the foot of her bed when something on the floor caught her eye. It was the little bear Greg had bought for her early Christmas present, a reminder of the baby they had lost. Last week her biggest burden was the grief she carried around after the miscarriage. What had happened? She picked up the teddy bear, and the zipper on its back caught her eye. She opened it up and pulled out the sonogram. His little jellybean. That's what Greg had called their child. He'd taken the afternoon off work to go with her to her appointment, and he'd been so overcome with emotion that he got choked up at the sight of their little baby's heart fluttering on the screen.

His little jellybean.

The memory of the sadness and grief following the miscarriage was still vivid, but it seemed minuscule compared to everything else that had happened since. Maybe Katrina should have told Nancy in the car. Never before had she been so conflicted, so desperate for someone older and wiser and more experienced to come in and tell her exactly what to do. She'd lived so much of her life letting others do her thinking and decision-making for her. First her mom, then her husband. It wasn't Greg's fault either, but she was so used to having someone else make up her mind for her that she hardly knew how to do it for herself. Her own hesitation could have destroyed her marriage in a single moment. Maybe it already had.

No, she wouldn't think like that. It wasn't as bad as all

that, was it?

In the end, she had done the right thing, she had walked away at the right moment, and she had remained faithful to her husband. Whatever test this was that God had thrown at her, she had passed it, and now it was a closed chapter. She didn't have to worry about what Greg would think because he didn't have to know. It was for his own good. Telling him would just burden him with one more worry. She wouldn't do that to him. Her mind was made up.

She carefully folded up the sonogram and was placing it back in the teddy bear's pouch when her fingers grazed her husband's letter that was tucked inside. If he wanted her to read it, wouldn't he have said so?

Then again, he'd never told her not to. Besides, she could use any distraction she could find.

She took out her husband's letter and unfolded the page.

Dear Jellybean,

Hi there. I'm your daddy. We never really got the chance to be properly introduced, but I saw you when you were about two months old. You were the size of a jellybean, and you were living safe and sound inside your mommy's tummy. There's something I should tell you about your mommy. You probably already know this, but in case you don't, she's the most wonderful woman in the world. She's my best friend, and I feel so lucky that she agreed to be mine. Losing you was really hard on her, and I probably wasn't there for her the way she needed me to be. To be totally honest, I was scared to death of becoming a father, scared of all the mistakes I was sure I would make. One thing that gave me strength was knowing that your mom and I were in this together. Even before we knew that God had planted you in her tummy, I was certain that she would make the most wonderful mother in the whole wide world. That's the reason she's been so sad lately, you know, because she loved you so much.

The good news is that I'm convinced that one day we'll be together in heaven — you, me, mommy, and any of your brothers and sisters that God might one day add to our family. No matter how many other kids God gives us, I know I'm never going to forget you or stop wondering what life would be like if you had lived a little longer. Well, buddy, I guess that's it. I'm going to say goodbye now, but I know it's only going to be for a little bit of time.

Love, Daddy

Ignoring the tears that flowed down her cheeks, Katrina folded the paper back up, careful to leave it just as she had found it. She opened the door by her nightstand and pulled out some stationary.

She had a letter of her own to write.

CHAPTER 71

"Mouse, I'm home."

At the sound of her husband's voice, she straightened her hair, wiped her cheeks one more time, and glanced in the bedroom mirror to see just how big of a wreck she was. With faltering steps, she made her way down the hall, trying to drown her nerves with an overdose of confidence and cheer. "Hi. Did you have a good time?"

He kicked off his boots. "It was fine. Nothing all that spectacular. Just handing out boxes."

She smiled. "Ready for dinner? I thought I'd heat up some chili."

"That sounds good. But first, I want to talk to you about something." He frowned, and she did her best to swallow down her heart which had leapt up and lodged itself in her throat.

"Talk about what?" Did he hear the way her voice squeaked?

He took her palm and led her into the living room. "Come in here. This is important."

"Ok." She wished she could pull her hand away so he wouldn't notice how sweaty it was. He didn't give her a chance but kept on holding it even after they were seated on the couch.

"I talked with Nancy while we were out delivering boxes."

"Oh?" For the second time that day, all the air around her vanished. She was dizzy. Could he tell how close she was to passing out?

"She said she saw you out at Baxter Loop."

"Yeah." Well, it was a good thing she had resisted the urge to tell Nancy everything. That woman was as big a gossip as everyone else in this town.

Was she really surprised?

Greg sighed. "I don't know what it is the two of you talked about, and maybe it's none of my business anyway, but she said something that really jumped out at me. She said it's hard being the pastor's wife at a church like Orchard Grove, but you were doing a really good job. And I realized that I've been taking you for granted. With the nursery and the pageant and my busy schedule and you feeling pressured into doing music when you don't want to …"

She tried to interrupt, but he stopped her. "Let me finish. I'm sorry that I've been complaining so much about things like the house and stuff like that. And I'm sorry for just assuming that you'll be willing to work in the nursery or play your violin or lead pageant rehearsals or any of those other things. And as far as what Nancy said …"

Katrina held her breath. Here it came. He knew about Miles. He had to.

"She thinks I should use my Christmas bonus — I mean our Christmas bonus — to take you to Leavenworth, and she knows of a nice B&B there run by a Christian couple, and before you argue, I already called and made the arrangements. There's too much going on between now and the Christmas Eve service, but we're leaving on the twenty-sixth and spending two nights there, and I even booked us the honeymoon suite. The lady I talked to said there's a big Jacuzzi bath. I want you to know how much I love you and how sorry I am to let work stress come between us like I have. What's the matter? What did I do wrong? Why do you look like you're about to cry?"

She ignored the tears that streaked down her cheeks. She had to do this. She'd rehearsed this dozens of times. She just hadn't expected to have this conversation after her husband showed her so much kindness.

Kindness that, as he would soon find out, was completely undeserved.

She took a deep breath. She could do this. "Before you

say anything else, there's something I need to tell you, but it's really hard and awkward and embarrassing for me, so I wrote it all out. I'm going to give you what I wrote and then I'm going to go into the bedroom, and I want you to read this letter and then wait half an hour before you come and talk to me. I know I'm making it sound really weird, but I don't want to be in the same room as you when you read it, and I want you to promise to wait a full thirty minutes until you come in. Is that ok?" She pulled the wad of stationary out of her pocket and held it out to him.

"What's gotten into you, Mouse?" He stared at the papers as if they were poisonous.

"That's another thing." She hadn't meant to make a big deal about this on top of everything else, but now that she'd found her voice, she wouldn't be silenced again. "My name's not Mouse. If you really need a nickname, you can call me Kat."

She stood up, praying to God that her legs might miraculously still support her weight. "I'm going in the bedroom now. I'll talk to you in half an hour."

CHAPTER 72

What had she been thinking? Why had she believed that waiting to hear her husband's response would be easier than having it all out in the open? It was too late now though. Just a minute or two after she locked herself into the bedroom, she'd heard the front door slam shut and then listened as Greg pulled the car out of the driveway.

She'd started a dozen different texts but didn't know what to write.

How long would he be gone? Was he so angry he'd stay away forever?

Why had she told him at all? What good did she expect it to accomplish? And why had she come up with that stupid *wait thirty minutes* rule?

She should have never let him leave.

She should have never given him that note in the first place.

The irreversibility of what she'd done made her sick. She curled up in a ball under the blankets and watched the clock.

Thirteen minutes.

Twenty-one minutes.

Thirty-two minutes.

Still no Greg.

Forty-six minutes.

He was never coming home. They were through. What she'd done was unforgivable ... just as she'd expected.

Fifty-two minutes.

A car pulling into the driveway. Headlights shining in through her window.

The sound of her husband opening the front door and kicking off his boots.

"Katrina?"

She had never heard him sound like that, so uncertain and pained.

"Katrina?"

She squeezed her eyes shut, hating herself for how fervently she'd wished for him to come home.

He knocked on the bedroom door. "Can I come in?"

She'd forgotten she locked it. The last thing she wanted to do was get out of bed, but what choice did she have?

"Katrina? I'm not mad." His voice was soft. She pulled the blankets off her and shivered from the cold. "I just want to talk and make sure you're ok."

She didn't look at herself in the mirror. Didn't want to see the blotchy eyes, the matted hair. How had she done this? How had she ruined such a good marriage in a single afternoon?

She unlocked the door.

"Can we talk?"

She hardly recognized her husband. Disheveled, frazzled, he looked nearly as awful as she did.

For the first time, she realized how thankful she was to see him. "I thought you were gone," she croaked.

"I just had to take care of some things. But now I'm ready to talk if you are."

She couldn't stop the tears from leaking from her eyes. He had been so good to her, and she had destroyed him.

"I'm so sorry." She sobbed out the words, waiting for his strong arms to wrap around her.

He didn't move. "I know. Come on. Let's talk out here."

She dared to raise her eyes to his. Was he angry? Was he going to tell her they were through?

"I'm sorry," she repeated, unable to take a step forward until he knew. Until he understood.

"We'll talk about all that. Come on. We may as well make ourselves comfortable."

CHAPTER 73

It was nearly ten by the time Greg stood up from his spot on the couch.

Katrina stared up at him. "So we're ok?"

He nodded. "Yeah. We're ok."

"You're sure you're not mad at me?"

"I'm just ..." He let out his breath. "I don't know what I am. I'm glad you told me. And obviously I'm glad you stopped things when you did, but ..." Another sigh. "It's still a lot to take in, you know what I mean?"

"Yeah."

"But I don't want you to feel guilty."

"Too late for that."

"Have you told anyone else?"

She shook her head. "I don't know anyone who would understand."

"Yeah, me either. But you know what? Nancy was saying the couple that owns that B&B, he's a retired pastor and she's a retired counselor, and they're personal friends of hers. She

342

said if there was ever anything either of us wanted to talk about, they'd probably be willing to listen and give some advice."

"Some advice would be nice," she admitted.

"Yeah, I know what you mean."

She twisted her ring on her finger. "Where did you go earlier?"

"To find out where he lives."

It was strange how they had spent hours talking about a man that neither of them was willing to name.

His admission didn't surprise her. "Did you find him?"

"No. And it's a good thing, I suppose. At least I didn't end up in jail." He cracked a smile, which Katrina tried hard to return.

"I'm so sorry," she whispered.

"You can stop apologizing now. I'm just glad nothing happened."

Nothing happened? That's not the way she would have put it. But maybe that was the only truth her husband could accept at the moment. Maybe it was best if he thought of it in concrete, black-and-white terms like that.

For Katrina, she knew something had happened.

A lot of somethings.

Some of them shameful, some of them not.

Some of them even good.

Like the fact that Katrina had told him to stop, and he had listened. After decades of letting others do her thinking, do her planning, even do her romancing for her, she'd finally learned how to seize control of her own destiny.

She'd finally found her voice.

CHAPTER 74

"You sure you're ready for this?" he asked as Katrina checked her reflection in the mirror.

She gave her peach sweater one last glance of approval. "I'm sure."

"You promised to tell me if it makes you uncomfortable, remember?"

She nodded. "I'm fine."

"Ok." He took her hand, she took her violin case, and they made their way across the walk to join the members of Orchard Grove Bible Church for the annual Christmas Eve pageant and candlelight service.

Forty minutes later, pleasantries exchanged, prayers recited, and carols sung, Katrina stood from her seat in the front row and stepped up to the spot by the Christmas tree.

Greg smiled at her. "This is a medley my wife has put together to help us worship God together this evening."

She gave him a small nod and lifted the bow to her string.

For a few days, she'd entertained the thought of singing

her medley, but she wasn't ready for that yet, and she wasn't going to push herself too hard. Besides, she and Greg would have a lot to talk about on their drive to Leavenworth in a few days, and she didn't want to strain her voice.

Tonight, she'd let Dmitry do her singing for her.

Breath of heaven ...

The lights dimmed as she shut her eyes. Faces in the congregation disappeared, her husband's last of all, until it was simply her and her music.

No, not just her and her music. She wasn't playing for herself any more than she was playing for her husband or the members of his church.

Tonight, she was playing for her Savior, the Savior who'd been born in a dirty, smelly stable to a scared and ill-prepared mother. She was playing for the God who had erased all of her sins and had convinced her time and time again over the past few days of his unconditional, eternal love for her.

She was playing for her Creator, who knew each and every one of her soul's deepest longings and promised to satisfy her every need.

She was playing for the Son who died on the cross so she could appear clean and spotless before him.

As she lifted her praise she knew her song reached the gates of heaven and rose like incense before the throne of her audience of one.

A NOTE FROM THE AUTHOR

Thank you, God, for allowing this book to come into existence. Also thanks to my editors and early readers and to all those who pray for my writing. I hope you enjoyed this novel. Although I've been a pastor's wife for over a decade, I'm thankful to say my husband and I have found ourselves serving churches far more gracious than Orchard Grove. If you are a pastor or are married to a pastor, I hope it was refreshing for you to read about a couple you may or may not relate to. I also hope that *Breath of Heaven* has encouraged you to pray for your pastor and your pastor's family!

If you're new to Alana Terry novels, the Orchard Grove novels deal with real couples struggling with real issues, but if you're ever up for a lighter read with the same setting (and many of the same characters), you might also enjoy the Sweet Dreams Christian romance series. In fact, book 1, *What Dreams May Come*, is a fictionalized account of the way my husband and I met. You'll meet Grandma Lucy and several other members of Orchard Grove when you read it.

For a list of all my titles, please visit alanaterry.com, and may God bless you, your family, and your church.

Books by Alana Terry

Kennedy Stern Christian Suspense Series

Unplanned, Paralyzed, Policed, Straightened, Turbulence,

Infected, Abridged, Secluded, Captivated

Orchard Grove Christian Women's Fiction

Beauty from Ashes

Before the Dawn

Breath of Heaven

Sweet Dreams Christian Romance

What Dreams May Come

What Dreams May Lie

What Dreams May Die

Whispers of Refuge (Christian suspense set in North Korea)

The Beloved Daughter

Slave Again

Torn Asunder

Flower Swallow

See a full list at www.alanaterry.com

Printed in Great Britain
by Amazon